A Pirate's Hostage

Carlotta gasped with the pain of his grip on her hair. "I will not talk of justice with sea thieves."

"Adam." A voice came from the door. Carlotta's captor let her go so suddenly that she fell back across the cabin.

The man in the doorway bowed mockingly. Carlotta had a confused view of a huge man, red-bearded, his sleeves pushed clear of his forearms, legs clad in hose of dark velvet.

"Forgive me, Muy Señora, if I do not introduce myself. Alas, our expedition is—" he paused teasingly, "illegal. You will understand me, I am sure."

"Only too well, sire."

He nodded. "You have angered my men."

"Give her to us, Captain," the smaller man whispered hungrily.

"Captain's privilege, Adam," the red-bearded man said gently in Spanish as if he feared Carlotta would not understand him. "Her jewels are yours to divide among the men. I'll choose the girl."

He lifted a heavy lock of her dark red hair and ran one finger along its silken length . . .

The Flight of
The Kestrel

Margaret Abbey

BALLANTINE BOOKS • NEW YORK

ISBN 0-345-25424-4

This edition published by arrangement with Robert Hale
& Company

Manufactured in the United States of America

First Ballantine Books Edition: May 1978

❧ One

MIGUEL DESIRED her. The fact had become increasingly obvious throughout the voyage. Now Carlotta turned her head deliberately from his burning gaze. He had been imbibing too freely and she had not failed to notice his hand was beginning to tremble as he lifted the goblet to his lips.

Her uncle shot a baleful glance at him before retiring once again to his moody survey of the cabin. Carlotta had learned to read his mind in so short a time. They would soon be in England and he hoped the onerous task on which he was embarked would soon be over. Her lips curled in contempt. The man was a sot. Her father had remarked on the fact soon after his arrival. Why then had he committed her to his care?

Her father's death was too recent a grief for thought. She caught the eye of her duenna across the table and rose to her feet. Immediately those seated round the table did likewise. Don Pedro Torquelo, the captain of *The Isabella,* bowed low as she swept by him. A junior officer hurried before her to open the cabin-door. She turned in the doorway, a regal figure, her mantilla brushing the actual lintel and bade them 'good night'. Her eyes caught those of Miguel again and she gave him a little half-smile. Her uncle bowed to her owlishly over his crystal goblet and she nodded her acceptance of the courtesy, then she was gone.

Teresa chattered brightly while she prepared her for bed. Carlotta gave her little encouragement. She tapped out her irritation with one finger on the small rosewood table-top on which her travelling mirror had been

set. She was tired, bored and sick at heart. She shivered
suddenly as her nurse swept down the heavy coils of her
dark chestnut hair and began to brush the long lengths
with an easy rhythmic movement. Her long, almond
shaped eyes sparked suddenly with greenish fire. They
were unusual, those light amberish eyes with the curious
green flecks. Her mother's had been blue, they said,
though she had had red-gold hair, lighter indeed than
Carlotta's own. Apart from these reddish, almost
mahogany-coloured tresses she had resembled her father. That high, commanding brow, straight, proud nose
had been his and the sensitive, well-shaped mouth. He
had been tall and unbending until the last illness had
brought with it a final stoop. She had watched him become angular until those high cheek-bones had stood
out gauntly from the flesh to give an ascetic, hermit-like
expression to the loved face. Now he was gone and she
could glimpse only resemblances to his features in the
glass before her.

Teresa paused in her brushing. "He is assuredly in
heaven, so good a man," she said softly.

Carlotta's eyes filled with relief-giving tears. "I believe it, Teresa. How well you know me. You read my
thoughts."

"It is not hard to see you are unhappy, Mia. Why did
you allow yourself to be persuaded?"

Carlotta looked up at the sharp black eyes in the
wizened, nut-brown face. Teresa was a peasant from the
flat plains round Madrid. She had suckled Carlotta
when her mother had died soon after her birth, having
lost her own child, and nothing could part her from her
heart's-love now, not even this sudden decision to send
Carlotta to the mist-ridden shores which her mother had
left as the bride of Don Carlos de Rodruigez y Cordoba.

Teresa sighed heavily. She had never understood the
master's rigid determination to return his daughter, his
only child, to her mother's land. During the last illness
he had been doggedly obstinate.

"I wish it, Carlotta. Your mother had been deeply

attached to the young Princess Elizabeth. Now that she is Queen in England, I am sure she will receive you at court, mayhap as one of her ladies. It is time you learned something of your mother's kin. She would have wished it."

To his wife's brother, Sir William Styles, who had journeyed to Madrid at his brother-in-law's urgent request, he confided his most pressing reason.

"She is too proud, unyielding. Her mother was a heretic and now that religious persecution is growing stronger and the King favours the minions of the Holy Office, I fear for her. She's not yet questioned her faith. If she does so and makes her own conclusions, she will never recant. I would she were safer in her mother's own country. You will take her? She has a sizable dowry, most of which can be convertible into gold and jewels and taken with her." Styles had agreed. He was a weak-willed man. He dreaded his arrival home with a woman so outstandingly lovely. His wife's shrewish tongue would not long remain silent on the subject. Her spite would be immediately aroused by the disturbing personality of his Spanish niece. He hoped the Queen would indeed accept her at court for a while.

Carlotta sank back among the pillows and watched through half-closed lids while Teresa extinguished the lamp, after undressing and curled up in the narrow berth opposite to her. The movement of the ship was not unpleasant though more pronounced as they neared the Channel. Despite its lulling tendency she found tonight she could not sleep and lay for some time after healthy snores told her Teresa was fast off. She listened to the noises of the ship, orders and moving feet on the decks above and the creaking of the timbers. She felt strangely at home on the vessel and was aware that she wished the journey to go on and on; while she was here in this floating little city, she could put aside the fears which had begun to assail her.

Miguel was her cousin. He was even now journeying with her on *The Isabella* so that he might join the staff of the Ambassador attached to the English Court. She would not be entirely among strangers.

She sat up and put aside the coverings, reached for her furred bed-robe, pausing as she sought her satin slippers to ascertain if Teresa had wakened but the snores continued unchecked and she padded to the cabin door and opened it quietly. The lantern above the lintel lighted her way and she climbed the companion ladder to the lower deck. A fresh wind was blowing from the east and she drew her robe tightly across her breasts and moved to the rail to watch the black oily waves below her.

It was becoming colder. She must go below. Turning she saw that Miguel had come up behind her. She lowered her eyes as she caught his, for once frank and appraising before he bowed his head to her, courteously.

"Is it, cousin, that like myself you found it difficult to sleep?"

"The wind is fresh. My head ached. I thought it would clear the vapours if I came on deck for a while. Teresa was sleeping. It seemed churlish to wake her." It was a tacit reminder that they should not be speaking together without the watchful presence of her duenna.

"My own head is thick with wine fumes. As you say the wind is freshening. We shall soon be in the channel."

She saw his hand clench tightly on the rail and she moved to slip by him to the refuge of her own cabin.

He put out a hand to stay her and her grey-green eyes blazed at him in the subdued glow of the deck lantern. "Allow me to pass, please, Don Miguel. It is late."

He bowed again, his own eyes dark with longing. "Forgive me, cousin. I mean you no insult. It seemed an opportunity to speak with you privately."

"But señor—"

"Only to assure you of my devotion." He was anxious to put her at ease. "I have watched you from a distance. I know you have doubts as to your future in a strange land. You have only to contact the staff at the

Ambassador's house in the Strand. The message will reach me quickly and I shall immediately be at your service."

Her eyes softened. "Thank you, Don Miguel, but my uncle has my welfare at heart, I am sure."

"Are you so?"

"My father trusted me to his care."

"The harm our fathers do us by their constant workings for our good." The whisper in the darkness was tinged with bitterness.

She caught her breath in a little sigh. She knew well enough Don Miguel was betrothed to the daughter of the governor of Cartagena. He had not seen the lady but it was a goodly match and the King himself had spoken of his pleasure in it. Carlotta found it in her heart to sympathise. She too would have preferred to remain in Spain, where life was dull and regular but pleasant enough. She had sworn to her father that she would be governed by Sir William. She could not now set aside her vow. She was as strongly bound by her love for her dead father as Don Miguel by the will of his living parent.

"It is true," she said quietly, "that I have fears for the future but they are natural enough. Sir William has promised to present me to the Queen's Grace. It will be good to know I may see you at court, and know you willing to aid me. Thank you, Don Miguel, I shall treasure your promise and hold it to my heart."

He reached out and took her right hand within his own. This time she did not seek to prevent him and he lifted her fingers to his lips. "You are very lovely, Donna Carlotta. I shall pray the Virgin to watch over you."

She sought now to disengage her fingers. "I must go. People would think ill if we were found. . . ."

"I know it."

"Good night, Don Miguel. I shall be glad of your prayers."

"Donna Carlotta—"

"Señor?"

"Think not the promises I gave tonight were made in wine. I drink to forget, nothing more."

He saw her nod in answer, then he stood courteously back as she went by him down the ladder and into her own small cabin.

🎀 *Two*

THE SEA was more choppy the following day. Teresa looked distinctly unhappy and Carlotta found it difficult to keep her feet when she attempted to go on deck. Don Pedro ordered the men to take in sail since they were heading into the wind and it was necessary to change direction and allow some respite from the severe buffeting *The Isabella* was taking. He growled low in his beard. He had hoped to be in the Channel by evening but this would delay them.

He bowed to Donna Carlotta, a gleam of admiration sparking in his black eyes. The two male passengers appeared wan and drawn in the morning's light but he saw no signs of malaise in her face, as she sat quietly partaking of a fair breakfast.

"It's useless to fight this gale. It may drop later today. You must be fatigued, Donna Carlotta, my apologies."

"I am not unused to the sea, Captain. I shall not fret at the delays. It gives me longer to become accustomed to the keener bite in the air."

He nodded. "When the spring lengthens you'll find the English countryside pleasant though damp and fog-bound at times."

"It is true I shall miss the mild air of Spain but they tell me the land in summer is green and beautiful."

"I have spent little time between voyages. London, I fear, is not beautiful. A stinking warren of buildings huddled by the river but I hear the praises of Windsor and Greenwich sung by some of my countrymen who served the King, when as a young man he came here as bridegroom."

She smiled, gazing beyond him. "My father came in King Philip's train. It was there he wooed and won my mother."

When he left her she sat on for a while but ate no more. Already the thought of her father and her longing for his presence now ruined all appetite. Had he been gay then, in the days he had first seen London and her mother, had walked in the Queen's train? Poor Mary, she had ailed always, they said. Well, the poor Queen had come too late to the marriage bed and King Philip had got no child on her; no wonder that he returned home as soon as he might and on the homeward voyage Carlotta's mother had journeyed as a bride, vowing that if the child she carried under her heart should be a girl, she should bear the name of the Queen's neglected sister, whom she'd learned to love in a burst of youthful confidence when that prim-mouthed, red-haired wench, distrusted and feared by the Queen and walking on a knife-edge of danger, had reached out once to take her fingers and sought her friendship. And it *had* been a daughter. Carlotta sighed. She *did* indeed bear that name, Carlotta Elizabetta, and now Elizabeth ruled in England. Could she recall, for old times sake, the friendship of the laughing girl who had wed with Philip's gentleman, and died so soon after landing on its shores? Carlotta hoped so, fervently. If not she doubted that her life in her uncle's house would be an enviable one.

She rose to return to her cabin. Teresa, poor woman, would need her aid for the motion of the ship had altered once again. As Carlotta reached out for the cabin door she was flung clean off her feet and fell heavily, striking her shoulder against the door post. Don Miguel stooped to enter the cabin; presumably he had been on deck. He came to help her, but he too only saved himself from falling by spreading out his fingers against the far wall of the cabin as the galleon shuddered and rose high against the crippling waves.

"Donna Carlotta, stay. Do not try to rise. I'll come to you."

He steadied himself with an effort, blundered round to face her and, crouching at her side, lifted her head and shoulder against his own body, to shield her as the ship keeled over again. She heard his muttered oath and put up her hand to her bruised shoulder feeling if the blow had caused her to bleed as she believed.

"Keep still," he bade her, " 'tis a long scratch only against the side of your neck. Let me help you on to the day-bed. God's curse on this vessel. Why do they not turn her into the wind again? She'll not stand this for long."

He breathed a sigh of relief as she sank back against the cushions of the day-bed and he looked round for some cloth with which he could dab at the wound on her neck. He took up an unused damask kerchief from the table and came back to her, almost sprawling on to her body as the ship continued to plunge.

"My pardon, Donna Carlotta. I can scarce remain on my legs."

She took the kerchief and dabbed at the wound.

"What can be wrong? I thought the Captain had decided to back into the wind, even though it was to lose speed."

"I cannot think, unless—" he broke off abruptly as Sir William Styles clattered down the companion stair and into the cabin, his face chalk-white.

"We are pursued," he said, reaching for Carlotta's discarded wine goblet and gulping, thirstily.

Don Miguel's dark brows drew together disapprovingly.

"Sir William, I beg of you, Donna Carlotta—"

Carlotta interrupted him.

"What do you mean, my uncle?"

"A ship is approaching fast. The Captain fears attack."

Again Don Miguel frowned. "That is nonsense. We are not at war and almost into the Channel. Barbary pirates will not journey so far into northerly waters."

"Not Barbary pirates, man, Englishmen," Styles snapped.

"I do not understand, Sir William," Carlotta said gravely.

"True we are not at war with Spain but there are many Englishmen who would have us so. They fear Philip and would clip his wings before his power is too strong. A band of captains," he snorted his irritation, "some term them the Sea Hawks, have leagued together with that scoundrel Drake to harry Spanish shipping."

"They would dare to attack?" Carlotta's face whitened. "But we carry an emissary of Spain to Whitehall."

"Aye, and because of it, I deemed the ship safe. Think you I would have sailed had I thought otherwise?"

"But why do they do it—the Queen terms herself a dutiful sister to Philip, in law."

"In open court she does."

"You mean she is not sincere?"

"God's death, Carlotta, are you mad? Have you no more sense than to accept the spoken word of princes at face value?"

He stopped, swaying on his feet as the trumpet above sounded, harsh, ominous. "A call to arms. Captain Torquela intends to stay and fight."

"And rightly so." Don Miguel hotly rounded on the Englishman. "Do you think we cannot dispatch a crew of rascally English scum from the river hovels and quay taverns?"

"Scum they may be but they fight bravely, as you will discover," Styles smiled, grim-lipped, his expression, for once, coldly sober despite the wine he'd taken yet early. "They will be well commanded. 'Tis strange though that they attack so near to English shores. The

Queen has forbidden these acts of piracy, sworn to take the head of any man found guilty of the crime, despite the loot in gold and jewels that yearly finds its way into the State coffers."

Carlotta's ears were strained for the noises above deck which told her the vessel was preparing for war. The men's bare feet padded aloft up the rigging. She heard the sound of straining bodies as men pulled on the ropes, and the cannon were run out, the more sinister swishing noise as the younger crewmen threw down the sand which would soak up the blood from fouling decks and making the craft yet more unmanageable for the fighting men.

The Captain came steadily down the stair and stood in the doorway to face them. His steel breastplate and morion gleamed coldly in the light from the stern-window.

"We are under attack," he said gravely. "I must ask that passengers stay below."

Even as he spoke a roar sounded from a distance and the ship pitched as the helmsmen sought to avoid the ball as it crashed towards them over the water.

Don Miguel stood up. The ship had slackened speed now and he was able to stand to his full height.

"With your permission, sir, I'll fight on deck."

"As you wish, Don Miguel, though I am commissioned to carry you in safety to London, and I request you bear yourself with caution. Donna Carlotta, you must go now to your cabin and lock yourself inside. I'll mount men to guard the stair near your door and you will not emerge until I send word that the encounter is over. I suggest that you accompany your niece, Sir William."

Styles nodded. "Come, niece, the Captain delays and is needed on deck. We can assist him best by obeying him."

She made to protest, then recognising the Captain's need, curtseyed and went past him with her uncle to descend to her own cabin on the middle deck.

Teresa had risen from the berth, her mouth slack

with fear, eyes glazed. Her greying hair streamed in confusion down her back and in the dim light from the port-hole she looked witchlike, unearthly.

Carlotta sought to comfort the terrified old woman.

"Sit down again, Teresa. The fight will soon be over. We are in no peril. The ship is well-manned and armed."

Sir William grunted as he slammed to the cabin's stout oaken door, and barred it.

"Aye, rest you too, niece. There's naught we can do and the ship will take a hammering."

He seated himself on Carlotta's travelling chest with his back to the wall while the two women crouched hesitantly on the berth.

They could hear cries now from the deck and movement recommenced with fresh urgency.

"The enemy ship is drawing close," Styles said briefly in Spanish for Teresa's benefit. "She'll be ready with grappling hooks to board us. 'Tis ever the Sea Hawks' way. The English Captain will not risk sinking our ship. That is a mercy, at all events."

"Sir William—"

"Yes."

"Is there real danger? Our ship is adequately armed, is it not?"

"Aye—but—"

"You fear this English ship will be the victor?"

"Unfortunately I do. These 'merchant' vessels are smaller and fast in the water, built for this purpose. Recently our gentlemen have found it highly profitable to fit out such ships and they attack only when they think they may do so with impunity."

"They will steal our cargoes, but what of us?"

He avoided her gaze. "That is why I said the affair was unfortunate."

"You are afraid?"

He grinned mirthlessly. "Most certainly I am afraid."

"For me?"

"For all of us."

She considered his words and paled but gave no show of the hysterics he feared.

He sought to comfort her. "It is unlikely that you will be molested. You are under Ambassadorial protection and you can claim the Queen's friendship:"

"To do so would be to exaggerate the importance of my position."

"I think it might be excused——" He broke off as the ship pitched and he was flung almost from the travelling trunk. Screams and shouts sounded on deck and an alien sound of grinding, dragging metal. Carlotta guessed its import. The two vessels had closed and grappling hooks clawed the Spanish galleon ever closer to the pursuing English ship. She heard Don Pedro's voice exhorting his men to have courage and to stand firm. The trumpet was again sounded and then utter chaos appeared to break loose.

"We're boarded," Sir William grated out between closed teeth. "God help us."

Teresa screamed and began to babble prayers. Sir William stood up and put his ear to the door. Carlotta knew he would have preferred to be on deck, yet understood his duty lay in defence of the womenfolk. He turned as the trumpet blew out a final despairing blast and the clash of weapons and shuddering crashing blows above stilled.

"It's surrender."

"Don Pedro has given up the fight?" Carlotta's shocked tones irritated him.

"My dear Carlotta, if he's to save his ship and the lives which remain he can do little else."

"Surely it would be more honourable to let us go down——"

"Niece, I for one have no desire to go down anywhere. Don't prate to me of honour." The sound of cheers and raucous shouting drowned his words. He shouted to Carlotta over the hubbub.

"They'll force this cabin door in search of jewels and plate. It would be useless to resist. Say nothing and keep calm if the men treat you with scant respect. Remember, we play for our very lives."

He stood back from the door as a splintering blow from a cutlass smashed the upper panel, following the sound of hurried feet down the companion ladder, and the door was flung wide to admit two burly seamen who jostled each other in an attempt to enter first. Carlotta rose with dignity and tried to disentangle her hands from Teresa's desperate grasp.

Styles challenged the intruders. "Get out, men. Can you not see this is the lady's cabin?"

The taller of the two slewed his head round to peer at the Englishman through eyes glaring from a face streaked with gun-powder, blood and sweat.

"This cox-comb speaks the Queen's English."

"You fool. The Queen's Grace will hear much of this affair, I promise you."

"Indeed, m'lord." The shorter of the two shouldered his partner aside and advanced towards the Englishman. His respectful greeting was heavy with irony. "And the Queen's Grace has a goodly adviser, I take it, on board a Spanish ship."

"*The Isabella* comes in peace. She carries personnel for the Court of St. James. Don Miguel Hernandez is a representative of King Phillip to join the Amassador's staff. God in Heaven, man, we are not at war. This is an act of rank piracy."

The shorter man's eyes blazed. Carlotta noted that despite his smaller stature the other men gave ground before him.

He came close to Styles and, leaning forward, seized the cloth of his elegant brown doublet between his two hands and pulled down Sir William's face close to his own.

"You talk to me of war and peace, Sir? If you would talk of peace, go out to *The Kestrel* and see the result of this peace. There are no less than thirty English souls on board our ship rescued but lately while they were in Spanish waters. Your countrymen—and you lolled in this cabin with this Spanish jade, while you knew what they suffered and you threaten me with the Queen's anger! God's teeth, man, I could run you through here and now and the Lord would judge between us if I commit mortal sin when I still your hypocritical tongue."

"If there were men of your land on the slave benches of our naval vessels it is no surprise to me that they have been punished as the thieving scum they are. It is by the mercy of Spain that they were given time to repent their crimes."

Styles's accuser swung round with an oath as Carlotta's icy tones cut across his tirade. He made a step towards her and Styles warned him, his voice now thick with fear and fury.

"Touch her, and I swear you'll die at Tyburn. Donna Carlotta de Rodruigez y Cordoba lies under the Queen's protection. Her mother was a close friend of Her Grace and Donna Carlotta travels even now to join the Queen's ladies."

The heavier man growled a further warning from the doorway.

"Careful, Adam. The Captain'll not stomach harming the womenfolk."

"I see no reason why not when it appears he is not averse to attacking a merchant ship on a peaceful voyage." Carlotta piled fresh fuel on the fire already burning in the other's breast. "Rape and brutality can be added simply to the count of his other crimes."

"The lass speaks our tongue, though with an accent," the older man commented.

"Donna Carlotta's mother was English. I tell you she is my niece. Her father is dead and she will now live with her kinfolk in England."

The shorter man gave a barked laugh. "She'll not enjoy it if she thinks to bring her Spanish mercy to English soil."

Styles released himself abruptly. He was white with suppressed anger but determined to keep his temper.

"Present me to your captain, man. I am Sir William Styles of Buckleigh. I wish to know what is to be done with this ship and the lives of Don Pedro's crew. Is the Spanish Captain yet alive?"

"Aye, more's the pity," the shorter man, Adam, snorted.

"Then allow us to proceed on deck." Styles indicated the travelling chests in the cabin. "Since it would be useless to protest against the seizing of our goods, take what you wish but, remember, I warned you. Those chests contain Donna Carlotta's dower and the Queen will hold you responsible for what is stolen."

"Doubtless our jailors here are likely to see that we do not live to prate of our loss."

At that moment Styles would willingly have torn out his niece's tongue. He gestured her to silence but she lashed out again as if to deliberately inflame their captors.

"Well come, you gentlemen of England, let us hear our fate. Do you cut our throats or leave us to drown?"

The man addressed as Will came towards her and she did not fall back before his undoubted rage. Styles advanced a step but the bigger man menaced him with his cutlass.

"Keep back, sir, or I'll cut you down."

Carlotta waited for the man to touch her and the seconds seemed to stretch to an eternity. She dreaded the feel of his hands on her flesh, yet she knew well enough she had invited his violence. He regarded her, his bearded mouth curving into a sneer. She gave back stare for stare, but in spite of her determination not to retreat she gave a sudden cry as he jerked out a blood-stained hand and, clutching the hair at the nape of her neck, forced back her head with such brutality that tears were forced from her and stung her lashes.

"What if your fate is not so quick, my lady? What if the mercy of we English gentlemen should allow you to live—to repent of your sins? What then? Our country-men served you, why should you not serve them?"

"You scum of the Thames bankside—"

Styles burst forward so suddenly that his captor's cutlass tore through the padding of his elegantly slashed doublet.

"Gently, gently," the older man warned.

Carlotta's tormentor ignored the interruption. "You will allow us the justice of the sentence, lady?"

Carlotta gasped with the pain of his grip on her hair. "I will not talk of justice with sea thieves."

"Adam." A voice came from the door. One word and in a tone which brooked no argument. Carlotta's captor let her go so suddenly that she fell back across the cabin, striking her head against the wooden panelling.

Styles appealed to the man's authority. He was in no doubt that he was now in the presence of the English captain.

"Captain—" he paused as if anxious for a name to be offered in introduction. "Your inferiors insult the lady."

The man in the doorway turned his attention to the Englishman. He made no attempt to give his name when Styles announced his own and that of Donna Carlotta and the reason for their presence aboard *The Isabella*.

"Captain, I implore you to allow us to proceed on our way," he said quietly. "Donna Carlotta's jewels will recompense you for the loss of *The Isabella* as a prize ship. I swear that if you do us no harm, no word of complaint shall reach the Queen from my lips."

"He'll not speak for the lady," Adam growled. "She's a taste for harsh speech and she believes in punishment. I say she should sample the brew—Spanish style, that which her kin deal out to the Indian lasses they capture."

The man in the doorway bowed mockingly. Carlotta had a confused view of a huge man, red-bearded, his sleeves pushed clear of his forearms, legs clad in hose of dark velvet, stockings and shoes of black. Though he wore no mask she thought hysterically he resembled the hangman ready to carry out his office and she stifled the scream in her throat and stumbled to her feet. Her head ached and she felt her hair sticky with blood from her fall against the panelling. Her legs threatened to betray her in a faint and she resolutely thrust her knees taut to hold her failing strength. He addressed her in Spanish.

"Forgive me, Muy Señora, if I do not introduce myself. Sir William has a point when he mentions the Queen's anger. Alas, our expedition is—" he paused teasingly, "illegal—a blunt term but one which you prefer, I am sure. We sail for profit. You have been outspoken in your opinion of us and I confess you are in the right of it. We are sea hawks, birds of prey, we attack our natural enemies lest they attack us—*before* they attack us, shall we say? I regret that my men must deprive you of your property. It is their due and I admit I cannot command them if I do not reward them. You will understand me, I am sure."

"Only too well, sire."

He nodded. "You have angered my men, lady. You talk of justice—reprisal—for us?"

"She talks of the slaves, Captain. She judges them."

"Oh—you have seen galley slaves."

"I have breathed in the foul stench of them."

"Aye, Muy Señora, you would, since they were confined in their own ordure."

"Filth they are, in filth they belong."

"Give her to us, Captain," the smaller man whispered the words hungrily.

"Captain's privilege, Adam," the red-bearded man said gently in Spanish as if he feared Carlotta would not understand him. "Her jewels are yours to divide among the men. I'll choose the girl. Agreed?"

"Aye, aye, Captain." The man stooped and seized the wooden box which stood before Carlotta's travelling mirror and at a gesture from the captain left the cabin. One more wave of the big man's hand and the second sailor followed, leaving Styles and the two women with the English Captain.

Styles made one final appeal to the Captain's decency.

"Man, you cannot—"

"Cannot, Sir William? What is to prevent me?"

Styles made to speak, strangled the words in his throat and turned away helplessly.

The Captain laughed and faced Carlotta. "You say nothing."

She shrugged wearily. "What should I say? This is naught but what I expected."

Styles moved to the port-hole. He spoke softly. "What is your intention regarding this ship?"

There was a deliberate pause before he got his answer.

"I'll allow it to proceed to the Netherlands. You will take ship from there to England, Sir William. I shall have leisure to dispose of the jewellery and plate." His lips twitched. "I shall keep the lady with me on *The Kestrel.* She will be my insurance, shall we say, that you make no complaint to the Queen's Commissioners. You will see that the Spanish Ambassador is equally silent."

Carlotta burst into a torrent of angry Spanish. "You will do as you think fit. The Queen must know——"

The Captain lifted a heavy lock of her dark red hair and ran one finger along its silken length.

"He knows well that if he does not heed my words, you will not be returned to him. Be silent."

"I will not be silent."

He raised his hand and coolly slapped her right cheek hard. "You lack discipline, mistress. Obey me."

Styles bit down savagely on to his nether lip. He moved uneasily but made no useless attempt to assist her.

She gave a sudden cry of pain, the second that morning, then checked it abruptly, disdaining to lift a hand to her smarting cheek.

"You do understand me, Sir William?"

"Aye."

"You will not wish to prolong the lady's imprisonment."

"No."

"Afterwards——" the Captain paused, weighing his following words calmly, "it would be unsuitable to present her at court. She will be returned to live with you quietly in your house in—Northamptonshire, did you say?"

Styles breathed heavily. He looked once at Carlotta then nodded.

The Captain reached out again to touch Carlotta. She flinched instinctively then conquered her revulsion and stood firm. He bowed mockingly.

"Will you precede me up the companion-ladder?"

She walked by him haughtily. Teresa gave a choked cry and sought to follow. The Captain signalled to Styles who drew the old woman back. She struggled in his grasp and then collapsed sobbing on to the wooden bunk.

As Carlotta reached the deck a scream of raucous banter greeted her. She gazed ahead steadily, refusing to look down at the scene of death and destruction. At one man only did she finally gaze. Don Pedro, his face white and strained, one arm blooded and hanging by his side, bowed to her gravely.

"Don Pedro, you are sorely wounded."

"It is naught, Donna Carlotta."

"Captain, we shall leave you your ship. With luck you should reach Dunkirk or Ostend." The Englishman spoke crisply in fluent Spanish. "The damage is substantial. You are breached below the waterline but you should be able to plug the hole."

Miguel stood by the poop rail. He seemed unhurt. Carlotta spoke to him. "Have no fear for me, Don Miguel. I am to be ransomed, it seems and I shall not—" she broke off, then continued bravely, "I am a true daughter of Holy Mother Church. I shall live until God and the Virgin grant me release."

A burly seaman caught at her young cousin as he strove to go to her.

The English Captain turned to the man, Adam.

"Are the goods transferred to *The Kestrel*?"

"Aye, aye, Captain."

"Then, Don Pedro, we will vacate your ship. Over side men. Grappling hooks away."

The Spaniard nodded grimly as the Englishman leaped for the shrouds and swung across to their own vessel in obedience to their Captain's orders.

Carlotta turned despairingly for one last sight of Teresa but before she could move he reached out and seized her bodily, lifting her without ceremony as if she were a sack of grain.

"Catch," he called gaily to the bigger man who had first entered her cabin.

Carlotta screamed and kicked in sudden fear and temper. She felt herself hurled through the air and landed smack in the seaman's arms, all the breath knocked from her body so that she was hard put to it to scream out her anger as he clutched her clumsily, laughing, though hoarsely in gasps as the wind was shaken from him by the force of the catch. Conscious that her skirts had been flung above her waist, revealing much of her silk-clad ankles, stockings, even her thighs, Carlotta sobbed out the bitterness of her humiliation as the older man hitched her to his shoulder and carried her below to the Captain's cabin.

✨ Three

THE SEAMAN stood Carlotta down somewhat urgently on the floor of the stern cabin. She swayed on her feet, then instinctively righted herself by smoothing her skirts and placing an experimental hand to the corsage of her gown to assure herself that her breasts had not forced themselves upwards from the low tightly-boned construction of the stomacher. Then she swung round, intending to slip beyond the sturdy, slower seaman, out through the door, up the stairs again to the deck above.

She could reach the rail, yet—the man was faster than she anticipated. He gave a low growl, put out a huge paw and, thrusting her back, went out himself slamming the heavy door to, in her face. She threw herself against the darkened oak panelling, clawing at it and panting then she heard the key turn in the lock and she sank down on the floor, her back to the door and gave a little exhausted sob.

How long she sat, worn out with her terror of what was to come and her fierce, explosive anger, she could not tell. Above her she could hear the noises which told her the two ships were moving apart, the clank and pull of grappling hooks withdrawn from the deck of *The Isabella,* the thudding of men's bare feet on the deck, the decisive shouts of the officers, then she felt the ship's movement quicken and knew that the Captain had clapped on more sail. She was alone on this ship with men who hated her for her race and her upbringing, men who had scant respect for her sex or the defence-lessness of her position. She moved wearily to her feet—useless to bewail the horror of her circumstances. She knew well enough all captive women soon learned to accept the needs and the innate brutality of men.

Her body felt heavy, leaden. She stumbled as the ship keeled into the wind. The cabin was smaller than the main stern cabin of *The Isabella.* This was a fighting ship built for speed not comfort, yet the small place was practical and would serve its owner well. The stern window lighted the cabin now only dimly and no one had entered to light the heavy lantern which swung from the oaken beam above her head, but she saw the shadowed sturdiness of the bed bolted firmly to the floor and nearer to the window the huge bench-like table which held the litter of maps and charts, nautical tables, ink, quills, dividers and compass. There was little furniture, two stoutly constructed chairs, a big wooden chest, se-curely barred and on this a mirror of Venetian glass in a gilded frame, its beauty incongruous in the bare simplic-ity of the place. She peered into its reflection, seeing herself but dimly in the growing dark of the cabin.

Her mantilla was torn and she lifted her hand to remove the ruined lace. Her hair fell about her shoulders
in a dark cloud. Her face loomed wraith-like in the fine
Italian glass, the eyes, huge and shadowed, revealing the
terrible depths of her fear. She frowned as she saw the
swelling which disfigured her mouth, giving it an odd,
misshapen form. Either the injury had been sustained
when she fell during the sea-fight, or later when the
English Captain had struck her suddenly, without warning and brutally.

The key grated in the lock and she turned sharply
from the mirror as the great door swung back on its
hinges. The English Captain lounged in the entrance,
his face in shadow but the light of the lantern he carried
glimmered on the brash redness of his beard.

"Hungry, Muy Señora, and in the dark too? We must
change all that."

He came into the cabin and, lifting down the hanging
lantern from its beam, substituted the lighted one in his
hand then he stooped and kindled the second one also.
She backed from him until she stumbled against the
bench near the stern window. The sound drew his attention and he grinned at her mockingly.

"Come now, Muy Señora, there is no reason to fear
for your life. You heard me. You are my bargaining
commodity." He paused deliberately, "Or is it not death
you fear?" He spoke in excellent Spanish with little
trace of an accent. He waited for her to answer him but
received none so he strode to the door and bellowed for
attention, this time in English.

"Peter, come down, lad, with dinner. Bring wine in
plenty and hasten."

She stood still with her back to the table, grasping
tightly at its edge with her fingers, till her knuckles
gleamed white and tense in the lantern glow. He moved
towards her. Reluctant to let go of the table she gave a
hunted glance around the cabin.

He continued speaking in Spanish. "Allow me, the
boy will want to set the table for dinner. Go and sit on
the bed," he grinned as she jerked her chin upwards

angrily, and corrected himself, "or the chair. Mind how you cross. We're running before the wind and the swell is high. Are you subject to sickness?"

She moved to obey him but without answering. He swung out his hand and caught her wrist in a cruel grip. "Answer me, señora. I am used to courtesy from my women."

She drew her breath in a sudden angry gasp. "I am not one of your women."

"Not yet."

She raised her imprisoned wrist high and dashed it down again sharply in an effort to release herself, but he held on tightly.

"You prate finely of Spanish cruelty, yet you have shown little respect for me, Captain."

"You are mistaken. I made no speeches about Spanish hospitality. I leave those to my men. They know more of it than I. I told you, I keep you with me to ensure that your esteemed cousin does not go immediately to the Queen. Nor, señora, will you, since you will have been my prisoner some weeks and afterwards you will be thankful to remain on Sir William's estate quietly rather than flaunt yourself at Court."

She wrenched herself free at last as the cabin boy came panting down the ladder with napery for the table. He was a shock-haired lad, tall and bony but clean enough. He avoided her gaze as if embarrassed by her presence in his master's cabin. The Captain sauntered to the bed, having stowed away the paraphernalia from the table in his sea-chest. He stretched himself out.

"Bring water for the lady."

The boy nodded and hurried out. Later he returned with an earthenware pitcher and pewter bowl, a coarse towel draped over his arm. He set the pitcher and bowl on the sea-chest and handed Carlotta the towel with a little quaint bow. She took it with a nod of gratitude and the boy sped off again, anxious to be about his business of fetching the Captain's supper from the galley.

She poured the water then touched her heated face and hands with the towel dipped into the bowl, dried herself with careful deliberation then sat down again as calmly as she could, on the chair. It seemed an eternity before the boy returned with two more seamen to set the meal. The Captain remained silent on the bed hidden from her in the shadows. At length he dismissed the men, rose and came to the table. Seating himself opposite to her he poured wine into a fine crystal goblet and offered it to her. She shook her head and turned from him. He carved beef and set a plate before her.

"You did not tell me if you are sickened by the motion of the ship, but I doubt that you are. You show little sign of it. Eat and drink. The food is good though plain."

Again she declined it. "I am not hungry."

"I did not ask if you were hungry. I told you to eat."

She met his bold gaze squarely, surprise widening those amber eyes of hers.

"I eat when I have a mind to, not at the command of another." She saw his eyes gleam under his heavy red brows. He was not angry, merely amused at her show of temper. He shrugged.

"Eat then at your own convenience but in one hour, if then, you have not obeyed me, señora, I shall force you."

Colour flamed in her pale cheeks and her eyes flashed but she made no retort. She took up the wine goblet and was angered to see how her hand shook as she raised it to her lips. His bearded mouth twitched but he too said naught and gave his attention to his own plate. The wine coursed through her, warming, heartening. She swallowed painfully when she once more replaced the goblet and took up her knife. It would be rank folly to tempt him to a show of force, and embarrassing in the extreme. She regretted her hasty words, uttered like those of a sulky child. Little though she relished the thought of food, she must eat, as he had said, and she consumed the meat and fine white bread. He leaned forward with a peach from the dish on the table. She obediently took it from his fingers, flushing as his touch, light as it was seemed to send a sharp tingle throughout her body. She lowered her eyes, intent on her task of peeling the fruit with the small silver knife set close to her plate. She noted it with interest, loot perhaps, from another Spanish vessel or a merchant ship flying other colours, acquired like the fine Italian looking glass which had surely not been purchased in England.

The Captain frowned as there was a hesitant knock on his door.

"What is it?"

"It's me, Captain—Adam."

"It is important?"

"Aye, Captain, it is, or I wouldn't disturb you."

"Come in then."

It was the older of the two men who had burst into her cabin who entered. Even without facing him, Carlotta felt the man's baleful gaze.

The Captain introduced him. "My mate."

She inclined her head.

"Well, man, what is it that can't wait?"

"Tom Pennyfeather, Captain. He won't wait. He wants to see you."

The Captain looked up at the mate sharply. "As bad as that?"

"Aye, sir. It is."

The Captain rose abruptly. "You will come with us, señora. This is something you should see."

Carlotta's hand jerked clumsily on the wine goblet.

"I—" she looked at the two men uncertainly. "I do not wish to go on deck."

The Captain regarded her for a moment, unsmiling, then he came back to the table and, seizing her by the arm, unceremoniously yanked her to her feet.

"Doubtless you do not, señora, but I tell you I have a mind that you shall see this."

The mate made no comment but stood back grimly as the Captain thrust her before him up the companion-ladder. She stumbled and half fell, catching her skirts in one of the lower rungs. He caught her beneath the arm-pits and pushed her onwards.

The deck was shadowed and she was breathing heavily when she reached it. She peered into the gloom and her captor took her arm again and drew her towards the starboard side, where she could see the gleam of a lantern and two or three men bending close to its light. They drew away at the Captain's approach and now Carlotta saw that a mattress had been spread under an awning and a man's pale, tortured face was illumined by the lantern's pale light. Another man crouched near his head and supported the sufferer's back against his sturdy chest.

The Captain released her arm and, kneeling down, took the sick man's hand. "Tom, are you easier, man?"

"Aye, Captain, the carpenter—he did his best for me. He's got a tidy way with him and knows a mort about herbs and simples."

"We carry no ship's surgeon."

"I know it."

"Now you must sleep. You need rest."

The sick man coughed and Carlotta saw a trickle of blood ooze from the side of his mouth.

"I'll get that soon, Captain, that's why I want to see you now." His claw-like grasp tightened and the red-bearded man leaned closer and gave his full attention. "You'll tell my Bess that you've seen me and that I love her still."

"Tom, you'll be telling her that yourself soon enough."

"Nay, Captain, you were never one to lie to a man. I'll not get back to Bess. We both know it. I'm glad to be dying on deck with my mates by me. Tell her how easy it was in the end. There were ten of us from *The Bridget*. Eight of us gone, five last voyage, three this. Bill died in the dungeons under the Holy Office. We came to think he was the lucky one. Now I know I am."

"Tom, you'll have no cause to worry. Bess is provided for and the children."

"Aye." The sick man relaxed his hold and sank back. Carlotta could hear his laboured breathing. It had been an effort to talk, but he was smiling. "I wanted to say thank you," he said at last softly, "for all of us. We knew you'd come—one of you." His eyes closed and the Captain looked up at the companion who supported his slight weight.

"Lay him down, man. Let him sleep."

"He coughs less if I support him, Captain."

It seemed for a moment that the Captain would argue then he nodded, and rose. "Don't let him exhaust himself. Are the rest bedded down?"

"Aye, aye, sir."

"See that they are well fed and rested. No man is to work this ship, till he feels he's strong enough."

The little group received his order respectfully, then he indicated that he intended to return to his cabin and beckoned to Carlotta to precede him.

"Let me know how he is."

Carlotta said no word as he moodily seated himself in the cabin, poured more wine from the decanter and downed it in one gulp. She had an unaccountable feeling that the incident she had just witnessed concerned her, though she could not imagine how. The exchange of words had been difficult for her to understand fully since the men had spoken in English and the dialect of the sick man was unfamiliar. She had caught the gist of it. The man was wounded and feared to die, yet he was old and sick. Why had he come on this voyage in such a state and why should the Captain force her to be present to listen to his dying words? She had sympathy. She pitied his wife, and the man should have died comfortably in his bed in England, not unshriven and unloved here on the cold deck of this pirate ship. She found the Captain regarding her intently.

"Have you any pity, Donna Carlotta?" He spoke deliberately, in Spanish.

She defended herself, her colour rising. "I am sorry that the man is sore hurt but he is not alone in that. Spaniards died—"

He cut her off. "You mistake matters. Tom Pennyfeather is not wounded."

"But—"

"How old would you say he is?"

She faltered. "I—I do not know, about sixty years or perhaps younger. He has lived a hard life—"

"He is twenty-eight years old. He leaves a wife scarce twenty-five and two young children."

Her eyes widened in shock. "But—"

"His lung is torn from the oar. He is spitting blood. The rowing bench claims its ninth victim from his ship. You heard him. There were ten. The other died under the gentle care bestowed by Mother Church."

She paled, her lips parting in the horror of the disclosure.

"Yes," he said sardonically. "Tom Pennyfeather was one of those pirate scum you told us deserved his fate. Well, señora, you may be right, but I'm glad I intervened soon enough to allow the last of them to die peacefully on the deck of my ship, breathing the air blowing off the English coast and with his friends to ease his passing."

"I—I had no idea he was so young."

"No, men age quickly in the galleys. Of course you may wonder why we left him there on deck. We could have carried him below. He couldn't walk you see. He'll not do that again, even if he recovers, which I doubt. His right foot is crushed and the rack has torn his hip joints. He preferred to stay where he is. It's less painful and the air's pure, as I said."

She drew a quick breath, angered by his judgement of her. "What I stated is no less true though he's had little mercy. He is a thief and heretic. Deny it if you can."

"I did not attempt to do so, señora. 'Tis you who passed judgement. I merely ask your opinion of the sentence."

"It is hard."

He smiled. "Ah, señora, that was forced from you but I am content for the moment. Now, I'll to bed."

Determined not to betray her fear, she caught her two hands together and held them tightly clasped on her knee, but she felt her courage drain away under his mocking gaze.

"What—what are you going to do with me?" She said at last. The words seemed stupid, obvious, yet had to be said.

He walked over to the bed and she strained her neck to catch sight of him. For some minutes he made no answer and she waited in an agony for some command to approach him. Her ears caught the sound of his belt slapped on to the floor, then the thud of his boots, finally the creak of the bed sinews under his weight.

"You, señora? I regret I cannot offer you suitable accommodation. This is a pirate ship as you constantly remind me. I suggest you stretch out on the floor or in a chair. It is as you wish."

She kept still with an effort. "You—you don't intend—" She broke off, close to tears of mingled relief and mortification.

"To rape you?" He completed her question and again she waited for his answer. "Alas, no, señora, do I disappoint you?"

She gave a sudden sob and heard him laugh in the darkness.

"I apologise if I reject what you offer, but I only have the taste for English lasses and harlots from the stews of Thameside. Sometimes I break my rule and take an Indian wench, but that's rare. At all events I find I need my bedmate to have a heart in her breast. You understand?"

She stifled her tears and went as far from him as she could go near the stern window. The planks of the floor were hard but clean and she felt safer away from the door where she feared the entrance of men from the crew. Crouched near the wall, she gave herself over to the luxury of silent tears, covering her mouth with a tight fist to prevent his hearing her. Her body shook with sudden fear as something touched her bare arm and she caught back a cry of alarm.

He called from the bed. "It will be cold in the night,

señora. I can spare the coverlet. Sleep well."

She lifted the heavy embroidered quilt and drew it round her. Beneath its folds she felt protected from prying eyes. Her body was bruised and aching and she was quivering from heat to foot. Beneath, the ship heaved like a live monster. Somehow she must exist through the long night of sleepless watching which lay ahead of her.

🎀 *Four*

TOM PENNYFEATHER died during the morning of the following day. The mate informed the Captain while he and Carlotta sat at breakfast. He nodded, dismissed the mate after giving instructions about the burial service to be held later that day, and she was relieved that he made no further comment after they were alone. He completed his meal and went on deck.

He had offered her no violence and she had fallen into a doze last night after lying wakeful for hours. At first her relief had been intense but now concern for her circumstances returned to haunt her. The ship would dock in England in one or perhaps two days. What then would be her fate? She knew well enough that after spending these days without her duenna on board this ship, she was ruined socially. It would be impossible for her to take her place among the Queen's ladies, even if that honour had been granted. She found herself worrying about Sir William Styles. Would he be safe on the Spanish ship and how long would it be before he ransomed her, if he indeed chose to do so? Her dower chests had been brought from *The Isabella,* and her jewels were stowed here in the Captain's cabin. She tried not to think of the gravity of her position, an orphan, penniless, arriving in this cold pitiless country without friend or protector. To whom could she turn if Sir William chose to ignore her plight? Don Miguel had promised his protection and her only chance lay in an appeal to the Spanish Ambassador, Don Bernadino de Mendoza, and a hope that he would acquire a passage to Cadiz for her as speedily as could be arranged. She had an elderly cousin in Madrid who might agree to accept her into her household.

The Captain joined her for dinner. She made no more childish refusals to eat and he was silent for the most part, preoccupied. At length he regarded her steadily and said, "I think it better you remain below during the service early this evening. However you've been cooped up long enough. You had better come with me up to the poop deck after this meal and get some air. It's fresh but fine. It will be rougher later."

"Thank you." She stiffened at his cool tone, but knew it was churlish to refuse his offer of protection from molestation and she needed exercise.

He gave her no assistance up the companion-ladder and she found it irritating to land on the deck scrambling and panting for breath. Two of the men turned from her to the rail. She was conscious of their contempt. The Captain guided her towards the second ladder which led to the poop deck and she lifted her skirts and as haughtily as possible climbed in front of him. It was good to be in the air again and once over the exertion, she walked to the rail and stared down into the green depths below. The sun was shining and the waves glistened but there was still a nip in the air and she caught her breath as the keen wind flattened her front skirts close to her legs, despite the wicker frame beneath and whipped at her hair, drawing out long dark red tendrils which fanned out behind her.

The Captain went to the helmsman and gave him his orders, then he joined her at the rail.

"Well, what do you think of my ship?"

"Excellently practical for its purpose," she said icily.

He gave a hearty laugh and leaned forward, his arms folded on the wooden top rail.

"We'll soon be home. See that faint grey haze on the port bow, your first glance of the Lizard."

She followed his pointing finger, and struggled to conceal her mounting curiosity.

"How soon do we reach harbour?"

"Some time yet." She knew he was being purposely evasive and she sought to change the subject. She had been so long this morning without company that she welcomed even his.

"*The Isabella* will be safe, sir?"

"I see no reason why not. The Captain seemed capable. She's crippled but she'll make port."

"This property of yours, where you will keep me, is it far from Sir William Styles's home in Northamptonshire?"

Again his bearded lips parted in a teasing grin.

"Aye, some distance away."

"Do you know Buckleigh?"

"I have seen it." He looked her over from her dishevelled hair to the low cut corsage of her gown, his eyes passing from the fine green velvet to the miniature on its long gold chain, which swung between her breasts. She had been wearing it when he forced her aboard his ship and it was all that remained of her jewels. The portrait was precious, painted poorly but recognisable as her adored father and set in an oval gold portrait frame ornamented with small pearls. Her hand stole to it, covering it defensively.

"Your father?"

She inclined her head. "He died only two months ago."

"Do not fear, señora, we'll leave you his portrait."

Her eyes glinted with sudden tears. "You are a strange man. I did not hear your name."

"Nor will not, señora, on board this ship. Some of my crew know me only as Captain, those who can put a name and rank to my person are bound by oath. They have been cautious for more than one year and many more voyages. They never use my name at sea."

"If you were known in London, would it be so dangerous?"

He was laughing at her again. He had left leaning on the rail now and stood, legs wide, his weight easily balanced evenly, his hands on his hips. She shielded her eyes against the light to look at him. Today he still wore a coarse white shirt loosely tied at the throat, full sleeves rolled up at his elbows, as he had done yesterday during the boarding of *The Isabella*. A simple leather jerkin, clean but worn in places was worn over trunk hose and stockings of black wool, and his hair concealed under a dark handkerchief. Was he indeed a gentleman? It was hard to tell since he spoke Spanish fluently though accented. Neither his manners nor his voice were like those of a gentleman. Certainly no grandee of Spain would have dreamed of treating her so discourteously but Sir William Styles had already hinted that Englishmen were less formal than the men of her own land, and that she must expect a laxness of morals at the English court which would never be tolerated between the walls of the Escorial.

"I could lose my head, or swing at Tyburn."

"But you must be known, recognised." She hesitated, "*I* know you, have seen you clearly enough."

"Ah, señora, I doubt that I walk in the exalted circles where you will be known and if our paths cross then I must pray that you will be merciful."

She averted her chin as he reached out and touched her cheek. "*You* can afford to be, surely, for I have been considerate—so far."

"You are a thief, sir," she said tartly.

"Of jewels only."

She drew away and went to the bows, acutely conscious of her rising colour. Her heart was beating fast and her breathlessness could not now be accounted for by the wind or the climb. For some moments she had allowed herself to be lulled into a sense of false security, now she was afraid again, as deeply as ever.

"May I go below?" she said quickly.

He made a mocking bow and made way for her to descend the ladder to the lower deck and called for a seaman to escort her to the Captain's cabin.

Carlotta prayed quietly in the cabin when the bosun's whistle summoned all hands to the deck for Tom Pennyfeather's burial service. Tears splashed on to her clasped hands while she implored the Virgin to intercede for the heretic who had died in the prime of his life and suffered so terribly in the dungeons below the Holy Office. For once the sounds of the men's feet on deck were stilled. She heard the muffled murmur of the Captain's voice and one final splash which told her the seaman's body, sewed securely into good English sailcloth, had at last been committed to the sea which he loved. She had hesitantly questioned the cabin-boy as to the reason why, since they were so close to harbour, that Pennyfeather's body could not have been conveyed on to dry land.

The boy stammered out his explanation. "I—I think the Captain would prefer Tom's wife not to see him. He is greatly changed. It is better so."

Carlotta was forced to agree that his decision was merciful. Tom's Bess would not wish to see her man, aged so prematurely and with ugly twisted limbs— better far that she should remember him as he had been, young, cheerful, coarse perhaps, but alive and loving her.

The Captain did not come below afterwards and when the light dimmed the cabin boy came and kindled the lantern for her. "Captain's compliments, Mistress, but he says he will send dinner for you soon and that he will sleep in the mate's cabin. I'll bring fresh linen for the bed. He trusts you will be comfortable."

Carlotta's dark brows rose enquiringly. "Then I am to eat alone?"

"Yes, Mistress."

As he set the meal he said awkwardly, "The mate and Captain has business to discuss, Mistress. We shall land soon."

Carlotta's lips curved wryly. Did the boy imagine she wished for his master's company? She nodded gravely but made no comment.

Despite the comfort of the bed after the hard night on the floor, she found sleep evaded her and she lay wakeful, staring up into the shadowy space between the beams above her head. It was stuffy in the cabin. The air on deck earlier had been refreshing. She rose and reached out for her discarded dress. Already she had learned to cope with refractory laces, but it was still a struggle. She looked hurriedly into the looking glass on the sea-chest. Moonlight flooded through the stern window and she had not wanted to re-kindle the hanging lantern. Her hair streamed down her back and she frowned. She could not pause now to dress it, but to appear so outside the cabin would be wanton. She looked round quickly for something which might serve her as cloak and hood since she had come on board this ship without one item of clothing from her garments' chest. The coverlet from the bed was large enough and would serve. She stripped it off and draped it round her, catching it tight round her throat with one of the metal pins from her hair, then holding the skirts of her robe and the coverlet high she softly tried the cabin-door. Apparently the Captain laid trust in his crew members since it gave to her touch and only the inside bolt had kept her safe.

The ship appeared to be riding at anchor, though they were still lying well off the coast. She saw the muted glimmer of lanterns on deck and quietly climbed the ladder, not without some problems with her refractory skirts. The gun deck seemed deserted. She gazed up at the helmsman on the poop deck but his eyes were turned from her. If the ship was anchored he was perhaps acting as lookout. She breathed in the salt tang on the air with real relief and made her way to the ship's side. She would wait only moments before returning below, but it was good to be up here alone.

It seemed suddenly that a cloud covered the moon for where the deck had been illumined by bright silver light, it now seemed dark and shadowy. She groped her way towards the companion-ladder, then gave a low cry of alarm as she caught her foot on a coil of twisted rope and fell heavily. She stumbled to rise but the noise had been heard and noted. There was a sudden pattering of bare feet and a lantern was thrust close to her face. She peered upwards at the three men who stared down at her.

"God's wounds, it's the Spanish jade." She had difficulty in following the man's odd English.

"What's she doing on the deck? I'd thought she'd be safe and tight in the Captain's arms."

The third man bent closer and she felt his foul breath on her cheek. "I'll warrant the Captain likes Spanish flesh no more than we do."

Carlotta strove to speak to them but they pressed in close. Now she saw that their faces were all set in lines of hatred. The man who held the lantern tilted it, the better to see her face, and she saw with dawning horror that his wrist was ringed with the red-raw scar of the galley slave. Only the chain gyves either on the rowing oar or in the dungeons had left such a mark. Her eyes flashed to the other two. The bones of their cheeks stood out sharply and their hands were clawlike, yet she saw the ripple of powerful muscles on the first speaker's chest as he came closer. The coarse shirt he wore fell open and she closed her eyes momentarily to avoid seeing the marks of the lash which criss-crossed from shoulder to waist.

He gave a grim chuckle. "I don't know, Job. Her flesh seems fair enough if she be a Spaniard. I'll not say no to it since the opportunity's offered."

The second man warned him in a hoarse, strained voice.

"Steady, man, the Captain allows no liberties on this vessel—so I'm told by the lads."

The first man chuckled again in his throat. "He rejects the lass. Why else is she here, alone, and if he does why should he object if we take his leavings?"

Terror caused Carlotta almost to vomit. She swallowed and forced her tongue to obey her. She framed the words in the unfamiliar English she had been taught since a child.

"Please, señor, allow me to pass."

Her tormentor gave a grating laugh. "Allow me to pass." He imitated her light voice, heightened by fear to shrillness, and the accent which lengthened the vowels unduly. Then he leaned closer crouching lower, so that his bearded chin almost scraped her neck. "And why should we do so, my pretty? If I had asked such a favour would my captor have obliged me—eh? Nay, lass, he said he required my services and why shouldn't we demand yours?"

Cold terror touched Carlotta. She stared from one to the other of the men, but they were concerned only for their own safety rather than any pity for her plight. The first man stood up and, reaching out his arm, jerked her to her feet so sharply that she gave a cry of pain as her twisted foot was jarred where her weight was placed upon it.

"Now then, mistress, let's see the colour of your flesh." Again he reached out and pushed back the improvised hood.

The second man turned from his contemplation of the far deck to give a low whistle of admiration.

"Such hair—on a Spaniard, it's like the colour of dark blood."

She shuddered at his choice of imagery. The fearful man muttered something indistinguishable and moved away from them. Obviously he had no wish to court the Captain's displeasure by any part in this little interlude.

Again the tall man's hands reached out. Instinctively she drew back, but he caught her by the shoulders and tugged her close, breathing hard, close against her ear.

"Do you know what they do when they fasten you to the oar, my lovely? They strip you to the buff and fling you a filthy loin cloth, all there is to protect you against the scorching heat, the salt lash of the spray and the biting rain you get in a summer storm. Months we've endured it and we carried a Spanish lady once. She sat under an awning on the deck lest the sun touch her skin. Has the sun touched yours, eh? Let's see it."

He ripped her gown from neck to the tight boning of her stomacher, tugging as the stiffened cloth resisted his hasty fingers. She screamed then and launched herself at him, her nails like claws to rake his cheek. She left deep scores furrowing his face but he appeared to be unconscious of the pain. She beat at him with her fists, screaming invective in Spanish. The hated tongue increased his fury for he caught her two hands in one huge hairy paw and pushed back her head until she thought her neck would snap. The second man also leapt to his assistance. He seized her by the waist from behind, and she fought a desperate losing battle.

Mercifully, as suddenly as her waist had been seized, she felt it released. There came a thud as if something heavy fell by her side. Her ears were singing, she felt herself fainting and as if from a distance she heard someone continue to scream. There was shouting, movement round her, then a stinging blow on her cheek. She felt it, cold, agonising. Abruptly she closed her lips and reached up a hand to the smarting cheekbone.

"That is better." The Captain's voice sounded far away but recognisable. "If you will stop screaming we can come to the truth of this matter."

She felt herself lifted and carried unresisting to a coil of rope near the ship's bows, then her head was thrust down between her knees and held there by a powerful hand. At last he allowed her to lift her head, sobbing and hiccoughing, but no longer likely to vomit or faint.

"You feel better, mistress?"

She nodded. Her throat ached too much to answer him. Now she saw that her two attackers were held prisoner by sturdy seamen. One hung limply in his captor's hands and she knew he had been downed by one blow of the Captain's fist. The other made no effort to struggle. He gazed dully at the Captain, expecting no mercy.

That the Captain was in a fury was apparent. His

points were undone, his shirt hung loosely open. He had climbed hurriedly into hose and shirt and come to her assistance immediately her cries were heard. He was barefoot, and had not stopped to seek for his footwear. Carlotta gazed up at him fearfully and pitifully attempted to pull the embroidered coverlet over the torn frontage of her gown.

He looked down at her impatiently then turned to the prisoners.

"Throw them in the brig, but treat them carefully. They've been ill-used enough. God knows, they were not without provocation. You, mistress, if you are recovered we will return to the cabin. I've no wish to continue to allow you to make a spectacle of yourself before my men."

The seamen pulled away her attackers. She swallowed and attempted to speak. "Captain—"

He made a further impatient gesture of his hand. "Not here, mistress, let us go."

She rose and the whole deck appeared to rise up and smite her. She staggered and would have fallen. He seized her, and, flinging her over his shoulder as the seaman had done when he first carried her aboard, dismissed his men about their own business and strode towards the companion-ladder.

Once in the cabin he hurled her on to the bed and she rolled over on to her stomach and lay there, clutching at the sheet, sobbing bitterly in her despair and humiliation.

He waited until the weeping bout lessened.

"I'll not ask you what you were doing on the deck. It seems pointless. You asked for what you almost got. It seems a pity I wasn't a trifle later. You might have learned a lesson but since you did not I'll have to instruct you. You made me injure a man I both respect and pity and to save you from your own wanton foolishness. Both men must suffer for the good of ship's discipline. I disincline to it since they've suffered enough. As for you, mistress, you'll not speak to one more of my men unless it be in my company and you will make no more attempt to leave this cabin." He paused as she made no answer.

"Did you hear me?"

She nodded, but her head was turned from him and he seized her shoulder and turned her face towards him.

"Do you understand?"

She gave one shuddering word. "Yes."

"Disobey me once and I'll whip you until you can't stand. I mean it, so you had best listen."

"I know that you do."

"God's teeth, woman, don't you know better than to walk unescorted among seamen or are your Spaniard acquaintances not men?"

She shook her head and choked on a sob.

"Get you to bed. Take off that ruined gown. I'll try to find you a fresh one, though we have naught on board to fit your fine fancies. I'll lock the door and set a man on guard. I'll speak with you further in the morning."

She did not lift her head as he went from her. She waited until she heard his feet ascend the ladder, then, dragging herself painfully from the bed, she divested herself of the bedraggled gown and coverlet and went to the water jug near the mirror. The moon had come from the cloud once more and it showed her a terrified, tear-stained face, and one livid bruise turning mauve and greenish along her right cheek-bone. She conquered her tears, dipped the towel edge in the water and did her best to cleanse her face and bathe her injured cheek, then she crept back to the protection of the bed, pulled the covers round her shoulders and cried herself quietly to sleep.

🏵 *Five*

CARLOTTA WAS not allowed opportunity even to speak to the cabin-boy alone. As the Captain had stated he made it his business to descend to the cabin and stand grimly in the doorway whenever it was necessary for crew members to enter. Once in the afternoon she was ordered to accompany him for air, above to the poop deck. He did not speak to her more than the usual civilities and she was glad to retire below quickly where she was hidden from the amused and scornful stares of the men.

As he had promised he brought her a change of gown. It was somewhat larger than her own, plentifully adorned with ribbons and laces and gaudy in its brash redness. She regretted that its colour clashed horribly with her hair, but since her own was ruined beyond repair she was forced to don it. As she stared down at its shining folds she wondered how such a garment had found its way on to this ship, from a harbour-tavern doxy's store perhaps. Carlotta's lips tightened as she considered how it came about that the woman had left her dress behind on leaving the vessel.

She was surprised when the Captain announced his intention of dining with her. He came dressed more formally in black velvet doublet and ruff, though his hair was still hidden beneath the folds of the dark silk handkerchief. She recalled that only last night had she seen him bare-headed, and then she had been far too bewildered to note whether his hair was red and curled like his beard or whether he was shaven-headed as many of the

41

crew appeared to be. He bowed with the courtly grace of a Spanish nobleman.

"Allow me, lady, to dine with you."

She curtseyed, flushing as his eyes passed over her figure clad in the shameless red gown. His lips twitched but he waved her courteously to a seat. She was conscious of the ugly bruise which still marked her cheek. His eyes lighted on it, noted, and passed on. If he were embarrassed at the injury he had himself inflicted he made no reference to it.

"We shall dock at first light, move in on the morning tide."

Her eyes brightened. Then her imprisonment would shortly come to an end. "We are in London?"

"Alas, no." Again he smiled as her eyes questioned him across the table but he did not enlighten her as to their true position. Peter came nervously forward to serve them and she did not press him.

The food was well cooked and served. Since she had been too ill at ease to eat much during the days since she'd boarded *The Kestrel,* she found herself unaccountably hungry.

He poured wine and smiled as she sipped appreciatively. "Falernion, from Genoa. I thought you had had enough of your own company, señora." She noted his return to his formal mode of address. Last night he had referred to her angrily as 'mistress' and 'madam'.

She cast her eyes down at her plate. "The time has seemed long."

"I regret the necessity to keep you cloistered."

"You will take me ashore?"

"Certainly."

She hesitated. "In this house, in England, you will provide me with a maid, some female companion?"

He regarded her, smiling. "I will see what I can do."

"How long—"

He interrupted her quickly. "Your imprisonment will be no longer than necessary, I assure you. I need to be free to go about my own concerns."

"To sell the loot?"

He bowed his mocking answer. She pressed her lips together angrily. This man always brought out the termagent in her.

"I must provide you with a more suitable wardrobe." He grinned wickedly. "The gown becomes you, but the colour is ill chosen."

"Perhaps the gown's owner had golden hair, or black."

"I confess I have forgotten which."

Carlotta peeled her peach with excessive ferocity.

He questioned her about her home and family. His sudden change from his tantalising mood touched her sad heart. She told him of her love for her home near Madrid and her longing to return, of her reluctance to obey her father's command. He drew from her carefully the fears at which she had only guessed which lay behind her father's determination to send her to England.

"Even at home my English blood is frowned upon. My mother was a heretic. She changed her faith when she married my father but he feared for me."

"And you are true Catholic?"

"Certainly, I am, a daughter of Holy Mother Church."

"It is nothing to you that those who do not share your faith are burnt in the grim show of the auto-da-fé?"

She faltered, unwilling to meet his hard eyes. "I—I do not know. If the soul is saved, what happens to the body is of secondary importance."

"And you think that God is served by such cruelty."

She was silent, uncertain how to answer. "The Church teaches that to doubt is to damn oneself everlastingly."

"You believe that?"

"Don't you?"

"I," he said quietly, "I believe in a merciful God."

When at last he rose to leave her he said abruptly, "See that your door is bolted. I have removed your guard. The men you fear have been rowed to shore.

You will be perfectly safe if you remain in your cabin. I will see you later tomorrow."

"Not in the morning?"

He pounced on the opening she offered him. "You will miss me? No, I too intend to go on shore tonight and allow black night to shroud my nefarious occupations."

Her face flooded with colour. She understood him well enough. Close enough in to shore, he would seek more congenial company than hers in a harbour front ale house.

Sleep came more speedily that night. Exhaustion took its toll at last and it was pitch black in the cabin when something woke her suddenly. She started up and pulled the coverlet around her, listening intently. The ship was never entirely silent. She could hear the usual creak of timbers and the lap of the steady water against the sides, yet above it all there had been some urgent sound which had pierced through her sleeping consciousness. There was no moon tonight and only gradually did she accustom her eyes to the shapes of the furniture and the pale huge square of the stern window.

Again came the sound, a quiet scratching against the door. She froze into immobility. Last night's adventure had taught her the lesson of constant vigilance.

"Mistress, come to the door and speak to me, please."

Relief flooded through her as she recognised the voice of the cabin-boy, but a second thought told her to beware. It was Peter, certainly, who spoke but was he alone?

"I dare not call out, mistress, please come close. Do not open to me if you are afraid, but put your ear close to the door."

He sounded more urgent now. She thought quickly. What harm could she do if she obeyed him? The door was solid enough and firmly bolted inside. She slipped from the bed, clutching the coverlet around her and stole nearer to the cabin-door. "Peter?" She spoke the one name, unfamiliar, hesitatingly.

"Listen, mistress. Can you understand me? I have little Spanish."

"Yes," she said softly, "but do not speak too quickly."

"You know the Captain is ashore?"

"I know it."

"The men plan to raid your cabin." He paused anxiously as no sound came from inside, even the gasp or hastily suppressed cry he expected.

"Mistress, will you trust me?"

Again she made no answer and he pressed on in desperation. "I can take you on shore now, to the Captain. There you would be safe. Do you hear me?"

"Yes." Her reply was scarcely breathed.

"Mistress, dress quickly. The men who plot against the Captain's command are in the forecastle. They'll down more rum before they risk the Captain's fury. We have time but we must hasten. I have a boat ready. The mate intended to be rowed ashore and then changed his mind. It is your only chance of safety. Mistress, if they burst in, they will—" He swallowed, too horrified to put into words what he feared.

Carlotta put a hand to her head. What was she to do? Dare she trust the lad? The Captain had forbidden her to communicate with anyone on board but the boy was right, she could no longer call on his protection. Even this stout door-bolt would not hold long against two or three determined men. She had seen their faces, read their purpose. If they seized her they would offer her no mercy. Tonight they would do what they wished and tomorrow face the wrath of their commander. Would he indeed punish them since his own opinion of her was poor enough?

"Wait, Peter," she said at last. "Give me some moments then I will come to you."

Her mind once made up she dressed with haste. Her fingers were clumsy and awkward, but at last she was fully clothed, her hair hidden beneath the improvised hood and cloak she had worn for last night's escapade.

In a fever of anxiety she drew back the bolt. It stuck

and she found herself in a sudden panic. Peter whispered an exhortation to hurry. Her fingers were clammy with sweat but she tried again. It seemed that the squeal of the metal as it was withdrawn would be heard the length and breadth of the ship, but no one called an alarm, nor did she hear the sudden clatter of feet from someone coming to investigate.

Peter's face was grim as he took her cold hand to lead her to the stairs.

"Keep tight hold, mistress. I will guide you safely, but tread cautiously. Watch out for rope, blocks and tackle on the deck. We have the advantage of time. The moment the crew hear the splash of oars, they will pursue, but first they must launch a boat and it takes time."

He guided her to the gun deck and to the boarding ladder.

"Stay still, mistress. I will go first, then follow slowly. Turn round to the ship's side and I will draw you into the boat. Have no fears. You are safe enough."

It was an agonising climb down the swinging ladder but she felt Peter's hands clasp her waist securely. The boat rocked wildly, as she seated herself in the stern. Peter cast off then took the oars.

He did not speak and she could see that he was exerting all his strength in the pull. The night remained dark and she thanked her patron saint, the Virgin St. Catherine, that this would enable them to move through the water less noticeably and possibly land unseen. She kept perfectly still, afraid lest she would make the boy's task harder, but she turned her head towards the ship, its outline now fainter, as the distance between it and the boat grew greater.

She had time now to consider what lay ahead. The boy had offered to conduct her to the Captain where he believed she would be safe, but should she accompany him? He would be busy with the boat. If she were to jump ashore she could run into the shadow of the harbour buildings. The boy would not dare call out since it would draw attention to them both and he certainly would be unable to hold off attack if tackled by even

one burly seaman and it would be more likely that the
scum of the waterfront hunted in groups. She resolutely
thrust aside the disquieting thought. She had left one
hunting pack behind on the ship. She was no less safe at
the mercy of passing strangers. She might find someone
willing to help her. True she was without so much as a
single coin, but she wore an emerald on her finger
which had not been seized with the rest of her jewels.
With this as bribing material and, if need be, the pearl-
studded miniature she wore round her neck, she might
obtain assistance in acquiring passage to London where
she could put her plea before the Ambassador, or even
the Queen herself.

They were far enough from the ship for Peter to risk
speaking.

"Are you cold, mistress?"

"No. I am quite comfortable. You are tired. I wish I
could help you."

"No," he was alarmed by her slight movement. "You
might overset the boat. We are not far from shore. I will
take you to some tavern and bespeak a private room for
you while I go in search of the Captain."

Her eyes gleamed with sudden hope. This promised
to make her flight more simple. This way she could escape without alarming the boy and she had no wish to
hurt him.

"That would be wise. I put myself in your hands,
señor."

She saw his teeth gleam in a grin of gratitude.

"I dare not return to the ship without the Captain."

"Peter, have you placed yourself in danger for me?"

He shook his head and rested for a moment on the
oars. "I know where to find the Captain. He'll not censure me when he hears what I have to tell."

A sudden 'halloo' broke across the water. Peter's
head shot up and he began to row more hurriedly.

"Boy—where are you?" The words were lengthened
out in an angry bellow, then less clearly, "He's taken
the boat."

"They've discovered our escape." Carlotta stupidly

put into words the obvious. The boy had no need of them, yet she found herself forced to say something.

"Aye, mistress." He gritted his teeth against the effort of rowing.

"Will they follow?"

"Aye, they will, and there'll be more to row. They can yet overtake us."

She clutched tightly to the boat's side, straining her eyes behind into the darkness.

"When I ground on the quay, you must run for cover among the houses. Tie up your skirts."

"But you—"

He gave a grim yelp. "They'll paste me, true enough, but never fear, I've had hidings before. Damn their eyes, they're gaining on us."

Through the water Carlotta glimpsed the lean slim shape of the long boat, manned by at least six men, possibly more, she could not be sure from this distance. She was no fool. It was useless to exhort the boy to greater speed. He had already done for her more than she had a right to expect.

She turned from the pursuing craft, to the misty outline of the harbour. Now she saw the irregular framework of houses and masts. They were drawing in between the merchant ships. Their black shapes moved restlessly, but silently, their lanterns giving but little light on the oily water. The men behind forbore to shout. They were certain now of their victims and no one would hinder them in their purpose. Carlotta heard the relentless plash of their steady oar strokes. Peter was panting with effort and she feared that he would tear a lung.

She gave a shrill scream as a rope snaked across from the following boat, missed her and the boy and was pulled up and back. Their own boat grated against the harbour steps and the boy sank down exhausted.

"Go, mistress, cry for help. It's your only hope."

She scrambled past him as now the men bellowed to her to remain where she was. She felt the stone steps under her feet. Her fingers grasped at the wall, slipped, and she fell back into the boat. The cabin boy called an alarm but the damage was done. Even as she struggled to her feet in a final desperate effort the boat reared away from the quay wall. Peter put a hand to draw her down to the far side to balance the boat, lest it overturn, but she thrust away his clutching fingers and launched herself towards the steps. The boat lurched with her weight and unable to save herself she was flung bodily against the stone wall. She felt the pain as her head struck, white hot, searing, then everything exploded in red fire and she fell into blackness.

🎗 Six

THE BLACKNESS which enveloped her consciousness seemed a merciful protection. One part of her fought against it, as if a yawning mouth was swallowing her wholly, while the less valiant self allowed itself to be drawn inward and held snug against the possibility of pain or terror from the outside world. Carlotta had never been a coward and she could not allow this lesser self to win. She struggled against the comforting, enveloping darkness back towards the light.

She was lying, tightly swathed on a strange, shifting surface. She could not see, it was still too dark, but she reached out, exploring with her fingertips. Her legs moved and dislodged the cloth bound round them. She was not pinioned as she had first thought. There was a cloak or coverlet wrapped round her. She could hear the sea. Painfully her mind focused on what had passed. She had been on board the English ship. The Captain had treated her harshly—yes, he had struck her. She reached up a hand to her temple and her cheek-bone. The flesh felt bruised and above her fingers encountered stickiness, blood. She had struck her head. That had been later. She had tried to escape. Someone had helped her. She struggled to remember—the boy—

But where was she? Was she on board the ship? There was the sound of the sea again and the cry of the sea birds but the waves were more distant. If only it were not so dark and she felt less sick. She rolled over. Beneath her the particles bit hard into her flesh and felt cold. She was not in her bed, nor even on the deck—but where?

Her hand clenched on a handful of small pebbles. She sifted them through her fingers and realisation came. She was on the beach, on shore. She had escaped from the ship, but she only knew of the boat and the boy—

Soon it would be lighter. She strained her ears but heard no one. On the shingle any one person near by would betray his presence by the slightest movement. She was quite alone. Why had they left her—and hurt?

She pushed herself upwards to a crouching position clawing round her like a blind puppy, but fell back on to the shingle as she attempted to rise. The air was warm on her face as if the sun was touching her cheek—but if the sun was rising, why was everywhere so dark?

With the dawn she would rise, make for the nearest house, ask for help—but if the sun was warm on her face it was light and she could not see—

She whimpered in sudden, terrifying fear, then put a finger against her trembling lips. She was not a child and she must not panic. She opened her eyes slowly, experimentally—nothing—opaque darkness. She lifted her face to the sky, opening both hands till she felt the warmth. She drew one gasping breath and conquered the desire to scream. It was true, she was blind—and here alone on the beach.

Now the full horror of the situation was borne in on her. She had no idea of her true danger. She knew she was probably on the beach by the feel of the shingle but it was just possible that she was on a cliff. Blind as she was, she could easily fall to her death if she attempted to move away from the spot where she had been placed. How long she had lain there she had no means of knowing or indeed by what hands she had been placed so. She tried to marshal her thoughts.

She recalled the flight in the boat. She had tried to mount some steps. Presumably she had either fallen and injured herself or some enemy had given her a serious blow with the hilt of a weapon or bar. Why then had she been left here? There had been a boy with her, Peter—had he forsaken her or had he been captured, incapacitated or even killed? This last was a sobering thought. What of the ship's Captain? Had he made the decision to abandon his injured prisoner, since she was dangerous to his security? If this were so—why had he scrupled to kill her?

Her back and thigh pained her as she struggled to crawl, her head ached though the bleeding had stopped and she longed for water.

She called as loudly as she could but her voice appeared faint even to her own ears, lost on the air as the wind freshened. A second fear assailed her. Here on the beach she was at the mercy of the incoming tide and it would turn—must turn, and she would not know until the sound of the waves came louder that death by drowning was imminent.

She prayed silently for someone to come to this desolate place, for it must be such, since there were no sounds of fishermen or the creak of boat timbers. It was terrifying to be cut off so completely from the world. Her prayers ended, she gave herself up to utter despair and sobbed in her bewilderment and fear.

So lost was she to her own suffering that at first she failed to hear the crunch of footsteps on the shingle, then her ears caught the noise of men's voices as they called to each other as they crossed the beach. The dialect was strange to her, but she choked back her sobs and cried out to attract their attention, pulling herself upwards and crawling in the direction of the sounds. The pebbles cut viciously at her hands and knees but she hardly felt the sting of them.

"Please, oh please help me." In her agony of need her English deserted her and she reverted to her native tongue crying and calling together.

The footsteps stopped but only for a second then she heard blundering movement across the shingle and knew they had found her.

"Why—it's a lass."

"She's hurt by the look of it."

She smelt the strong fishy odour as they bent over her and judged them fishermen come to tend their nets.

"Steady, lass." One man stooped to touch her shoulder. She sobbed out her story—a strange mixture of Spanish and English and she knew in the end by their puzzled silence that they did not understand her.

She clutched despairingly at the rough wollen sleeve. "You must help me. I cannot see."

"The lass is foreign." One of the men sounded doubtful. "Italian do you think or Spanish?"

"She's blind." The other man bent over her. She felt his breath on her cheek. "She hit her temple. See the wound, Tom? Sir Robin is riding near the dunes. Give him a call. I'll stay with the lass."

He soothed her as gently as he could. "Rest back, mistress. None here will hurt thee. Try to keep calm while we fetch help."

She strove to thank him but words eluded her and she sank back against his sturdy frame while he knelt on the shingle beside her and his great rough hand stroked her arm in an effort to comfort.

There was a quick flurry of movement and the pebbles scudded and Carlotta knew the summoned rider approached. She turned her head towards the sound. A man came towards them, walking lightly.

"What's this, Harry?" The voice was light, pleasant, more cultured, but that of a complete stranger.

"It's a lass, sir, from the sea. I cannot say how she came here. She makes no sense."

"Stay back, man, and let me see."

The newcomer sank down on one knee and took Carlotta's hand in his own. "Now, do not be afraid." He squeezed the hand gently as if to reassure her if his words could not. "Did you say she was foreign, Tom?"

The man's voice sounded doubtful. "I suspect she's Spanish, sir, from what she jabbered just now. I've heard one or two words in the tongue. My brother was held captive for some days after Cadiz and he picked up one or two bits of the language. What I can't understand is how she got here. She can't walk. She's blind and no ship has been sighted."

The man in authority spoke to her slowly in English. "Can you understand us? We do not speak your tongue."

"Yes—yes." Excitement threatened to defeat her effort and he placed a hand gently over her mouth.

"Don't try to talk yet. Trust us. You are safe. I shall carry you up the beach. There's a fisherman's hut where you can rest."

"Please, please—" Carlotta whispered to him urgently and he bent his ear close to her lips.

"Tell me, señor, is my dress torn? Am I decently clad?"

He was quick to reassure her.

"Certainly you are."

She fell back relieved as he lifted her without apparent effort and walked back up the beach.

"Harry, bring my horse—no, better still, ride to the house and give orders for them to send a litter and warm blankets. Tell Tom to get me some water from the spring."

Harry murmured his acquiescence and Carlotta conquered her tears as she felt the man stoop and enter some low doorway. He placed her carefully down on some dry wooden planking.

"Lie still for a moment. Help is at hand. When you have had some water and I've cleaned this wound you can talk, if you can."

When the fisherman returned with a pannikin of water she drank thirstily and she felt her rescuer's gentle fingers explore the wound on her temple. He bathed it with a dampened cloth, presumably his kerchief, since it smelt clean and faintly of some perfumed or spiced fragrance.

"You say you can see nothing?" He enquired gently.

"Nothing. I—"

"You have always been blind?"

"No—I had some accident. I fell—"

"I understand. Do not disturb yourself yet. This state is possibly only temporary. Can you understand that? Soon you will see again. We will take you to my house and summon my physician. For the present it is best that you lie quiet. Answer me one question only. Are you Spanish? What is your name?"

"Carlotta Elizabetta de Rodruigez y Cordoba. My father was Spanish but my mother was the sister of Sir William Styles of Buckleigh in Northamptonshire."

"Ah, I think I begin to see light. Do not worry any more. Your uncle will be informed of your injury. He will be brought to Priors Mallory. My people will tell him you are there when he searches for you."

"Priors—" She tried to repeat the name, puzzled.

"My house is called Priors Mallory. I am Sir Robin Mallory. The house is only a mile or so away. When the litter arrives we will take you there."

"This house, where is it—in London?"

"London?" His light voice betrayed surprise. "Why no. Did you think yourself near London? You are in Norfolk near the port of Lynn—King's Lynn."

"King's Lynn," she spoke the name slowly. It was utterly unknown to her. So *The Kestrel* was in Lynn Harbour, or had it landed her there and sailed on? She was bewildered by the helplessness of her plight but too exhausted to question further. She lay back on the floor while Sir Robin placed something warm and soft beneath her head. For the moment she was content to leave all matters in this man's capable hands. He seemed kind. She must trust him since no other course was open to her.

When the litter arrived Sir Robin lifted her bodily and wrapped her warmly in the blankets. Though the sun shone warm on her face, she was shivering violently and her teeth chattered. She was glad to feel the security of the warmth and the pleasant slow movement of the litter lulled her into a state of partial relaxation.

When the litter was halted she jerked up her head anxiously. Now she was surrounded by alien sounds, the barking of excited dogs, the creak and jingle of harness, the clanking of pails and a great deal of chatter which was hushed by Sir Robin's cautious but determined demand for quiet. He came to the side of the litter and touched her hand.

"We have arrived at Priors Mallory, Donna Carlotta. As its owner I bid you welcome. Here is my housekeeper, Martha Wagg. She is an excellent, practical female and I shall place you in her hands." He called an order to his groom and then stooped and lifted her once more.

She was relieved that he did her this service since each strange presence was bewildering and frightening and she had become accustomed to the feel and fresh scent of his velvet doublet against her cheek.

She knew that he climbed slowly what seemed a short set of stairs. A woman's voice murmured something she could not catch, then she found herself lowered on to a wide soft bed. Sir Robin drew away to give instructions to his servant and she lay still, clutching at the cool linen sheet beneath her.

Her hearing already appeared more acute and she caught what he said.

"I've sent Job Harris for Dr. Hartington. Undress her and make her comfortable. Poor lady, she is terrified. Do not press her to talk. In all events she knows little. Speak slowly."

"I will sir."

Carlotta was concerned that her one link with reality was leaving her, but she controlled her shaking to thank him.

"Thank you so very much, señor. I have nothing with which to pay you or the physician but—"

He cut her short firmly. "You will not insult us, Donna Carlotta. My hospitality is entirely at your disposal, until we are in communication with your uncle. I will not press you for your story. Martha will make you comfortable. When the doctor has left, you must sleep."

He moved away again before she could answer and the woman came to her side, when the door closed behind him.

From her voice Carlotta judged her to be elderly. She was brisk and her kindly tones were countrified but just comprehensible.

"Now, my lovely, let Martha help you from this dirty gown and you shall wear one of the mistress's shifts. Mary," she addressed someone behind who entered walking heavily as if burdened with some weighty object, "put the pail of hot water down and leave me with our guest. I can manage alone. It is better so, but bring me some fresh bread and mulled ale—aye, and some white chicken meat, from the breast and some syllabub. Get cook to be quick now."

Carlotta allowed herself to be undressed and washed like a child. Afterwards, when the clean lavender-scented sheets were drawn up to her chin, she found herself crying quietly in spite of her determination not to do so.

"Now, now, my lady, there's naught to fret about. I'll not leave you."

"I am so helpless—" Carlotta sought for English words to express herself. "You are all so kind but I fear."

"I know, but believe me Sir Robin will do everything for your well-being and comfort. You can trust him."

There was an authoritative knock on the door.

"That will be Dr. Hartington. He'll dress your wounds and you'll feel better."

Carlotta had expected some elderly learned man, for all the physicians and surgeons of her acquaintance had been so but the firm clasp of the man's hand on her fingers dispelled any such notions.

"Can you answer me in English, mistress? If not I have some Spanish. Sir Robin tells me you are from Spain."

"I speak English well, sir, and I must now that I am here in your land."

"Good. Clench your hand tightly—pull against my fingers. So, that is good, not too weak. They tell me you fell and now cannot see. This is a deep gash." His fingers explored the wound as Sir Robin had done. "How was this?"

She caught back a sob. "I do not know. I tried to climb from a boat, I think—but I cannot remember— I—I hit my head on the wall—"

"Against the quay, perhaps. The bruising is bad on the cheek-bone too."

She was about to explain about that blow and thought better of it.

"I will dress the wound for you. Martha, pull back the sheets. Let us assure ourselves that Donna Carlotta has taken no other hurt."

When he had completed his examination, he said, "I will leave you a draught which will help you to sleep. There are no broken bones and the cut will heal. The scar will be no detriment to your beauty."

"But my eyes—will I see?"

His reply was more cautious. "I think you will do so in time. I have seen such blindness before which has cured itself. The blow was severe. We can only hope. Try not to distress yourself. Nature is the best healer. You are in good hands. I will see you again tomorrow. Martha will summon me if there is need. Try to eat and then sleep—that is essential for your well-being."

"I vow—" she corrected herself. "I will promise, is that correct—to try."

Martha conducted him from the room. Carlotta lifted her fingers and touched her closed eyelids, she blinked her lashes rapidly and felt the tears wet on her finger-tips. The linen bandage round her temple felt cool and

exuded a strange aromatic smell from the ointment he
had used. The wound pained her less, but her despair
was pitiful. This man seemed so cool, so formal. He
gave her little hope that she would ever be anything but
a helpless beggar and since her dower was lost to her,
utterly dependent on the charity of strangers.

Martha scolded her roundly. "Tears again? You will
make your eyes red, my lovely. Let Martha help you to
sit up and you must try to eat a little.

"There, that is better. I'll mix you the doctor's physic
and you must sleep. I'll stay by you all the time and
tonight I'll sleep here in case you have need of me."

Carlotta sank back against her pillows. "Will not
your mistress have need of you?"

"Mistress? Nay, lady. There's no mistress here but
old Martha."

"Is Sir Robin then, not married?"

"Not yet. I'm sick of urging him to take a wife,
though he'll doubtless bring some flibberty gibbet here
who'll lord it over me."

She laughed at Carlotta's puzzlement. "It's not a
word you know, lady. I'll make it clear—pretty and
without a brain in her head."

"But my shift?"

"Belonged to Sir Robin's mother, but she died almost
two years ago. She ailed for long years, poor lady. As
for his father, Sir Harry was killed hunting boar some
eight years since."

The doctor's draught was somewhat bitter but Carlotta swallowed it obediently. The old woman's gossip
made her drowsy and the food and wine had strength-
ened her. She slipped at last into a dream-filled sleep in
which boys with red beards flourishing cutlasses menaced her and boats reared their bows to strike her un-
protected head. She woke once, crying out in stark terror. Immediately she heard the housekeeper's padding
footsteps and the woman's quiet reassurance.

"All is well, lady. It is night. You've had a bad
dream. You are here safe at Priors Mallory. The household is abed but Martha is close."

Carlotta reached out for the woman's horny hand. She gave a little sigh and settled herself once more on the pillows. At last she slept, this time mercifully without dreams.

Seven

THE BARKING of the dogs from the courtyard below woke her. She opened her eyes expecting to see the sun come dazzling through the casement and the first shock of realisation that she was still blind hit her again like a physical blow. She pawed about her in the great bed and called out.

"Martha?"

For once her nurse and protector had left her side and she sat up turning her head to one side and then the other for a clue as to the geography of the room. From her left she could detect a faint sound as if a curtain moved in the breeze from the window. She pushed back the covers and tried to stand up, reaching out blindly and encountering the stolid thickness of the bed post on which to trust her weight. So far so good. She wanted to go to the window to feel the sun on her face, and the air. The continued joyful barking of the dogs told her the day was fine and that the master was probably close-by. She let go of the post and ventured forward, both arms extended before her to feel her way. Disaster overtook her after only one or two steps. Her foot struck some object, a stool perhaps, and she came down heavily on to the carpet. The door opened and Martha gave an alarmed cry from behind her.

"Lady, you should not. Come back to bed at once

and have breakfast. You must not attempt to get up until the doctor has been."

Ruefully Carlotta scrambled to her feet.

"Martha, I am not ill—not hurt. I must try to learn what is in the room. I will bump my head and my knees—so, what of that? I cannot lie in bed all the day. Take me, please, to the window and then I will eat your so fine breakfast."

The old woman grumbled but put down the tray. "Keep still one moment while I put on this bed gown. You must come afterwards to bed. You promise?"

"Tell me what is below? Be my eyes, Martha. I can hear the dogs. Is Sir Robin there?"

"Not now. He came in some minutes ago from riding. The spaniels are demanding admittance. He spoils them. Patch is black and white—the bitch—and Kendall is black, a beauty."

"This is the courtyard?"

"Yes, on the right the stables and outbuildings and further off the dairy, buttery and can you hear the doves? The dovecote is here in the courtyard. Behind is the herb garden but the beauty of the house lies in the knot garden. When you are well you must sit there and enjoy the scent of the flowers. The roses and lilies will soon be out and—" She hesitated, unwilling to put into words the thought that if the Spanish beauty would not by then be capable of seeing their splendour of colour the fragrance of the summer flowers and climbing wisteria and the lilac near the wall would still give some delight. Anxious to change the subject she said coaxingly, "You promised to return to bed. Come and eat, then I will make you ready for visitors."

"The doctor?"

"Sir Robin has asked that he might pay his respects and I am to tell him when you will receive him. Master Martyn will come later."

"Master Martyn?"

"I still call Dr. Hartington that. He will always be young Master Martyn to me I reckon, as often I call Sir Robin young master."

"The doctor has always lived in these parts then?"

"Bless you, yes. He has been a friend of Sir Robin's since childhood. He's the son of the rector."

Carlotta pondered on the information she'd received about the household while Martha assisted her to eat. After the housekeeper had washed her and dressed her hair, she sat propped up by the pillows and expressed herself anxious to receive her host.

He came to her side with firm but slow steps so as not to alarm her. "Martha tells me you are better."

"I am so. You have all of my gratitude, sir. Had not you—"

"We will not speak of that. The doctor told me he has high hopes that you will recover fully, but you must not distress yourself. Rest, eat, be lazy and trust us. I have sent a messenger both to Buckleigh and to the Queen, whose Ambassador must be informed. For the present you are amply chaperoned by Martha's presence here, but I would be glad if now you can bring yourself to tell me your story. Are you well enough?"

"I am, sir, but—" she faltered and he waited patiently. "I think the head blow has caused me to forget some of what happened. I am confused."

"Give me what facts you remember. Do not hurry. There is plenty of time. Things may come back to you during the next few days. In the meantime I must be knowledgeable so that I can help you."

She told him the story with pitiful simplicity. Sometimes words failed her and she needed to grope for expressions unknown to her in English, but already fluency was returning. Her father had spoken to her constantly in her mother's tongue and her journey with Sir William Styles had made it more familiar. Her immediate concern was for her uncle's safety and to be reassured about the fate of the boy who had helped her.

"Then the last thing you recall is the flight in the boat from this ship—*The Kestrel?*"

She nodded. "We had reached the quay and the long boat caught up. They threw a rope or grappling hook. I think I tried to climb a ladder—" She broke off and shook her head. "When I woke I was on the beach and—" her lip trembled, "I—I could not see."

He said nothing for some moments and she knew he was considering deeply.

"This pirate, if he is found—he will be punished?"

"Assuredly. We must do our best to bring him to justice. By this unprecedented attack on the Spanish ship he brings our country periously close to war. God knows the Queen has striven constantly for years to avoid open conflict with His Catholic Majesty."

"Unlike most English then you counsel peace?"

He gave a light laugh. "My dear Donna Carlotta, when you know me better I'm afraid you will censure me for cowardice. I am for peace at any price—always."

"But the ship *The Kestrel?*"

She almost felt his shrug so rueful was his tone. "A common enough bird of prey. Many ships are so named. In this way its anonymity is assured. You say yourself the Captain's name was never mentioned in your presence."

"The cabin boy was Peter and the mate I think, Adam."

"Both names common in England. Again such information would gain us little. Our chief hope lies in the fact that you would know the man again if you saw him. You did see him clearly?"

She coloured hotly. "Indeed. We cannot discount the fact that I may never see him, Sir Robin."

"Quite so." His answer was direct. He made no effort to dissimulate. "But presumably your uncle saw him and your cousin, Don Miguel, was it?"

"For moments only in the heat of the battle and just after."

"Yes, of course the fellow is unlikely to cross your circle of acquaintances. Don Miguel will join the Court and Sir William is a wealthy man—"

"But Sir William said many English gentlemen enrich their coffers by such means."

"By proxy only." He laughed. "Few of our Court

gallants will venture themselves at sea or in attack. Like me they prefer the comforts of their own firesides and their most hazardous enterprise is in the boar hunt. No, Donna Carlotta, I think we are unlikely to find your rascally Captain at court."

"But *The Kestrel,* is she not in harbour at Lynn?"

"No, I have already made enquiries about all ships in the hopes I might discover how you had landed on the beach, even before I knew of the attack on your ship. There is no such vessel as you describe in the port. To that I will swear. You do not know how long since you were hurt. The accident may have occured at any port along the coast."

"I had no thought of that, but the boy, will you make enquiries about the lad?"

"I will indeed, though I think it unlikely I shall have any success."

"You mean they will have killed him?"

He was cautious. "It is very possible or he may have been returned to the ship."

He rose and spoke to Martha who had remained near to the window during their talk. "Will you fetch Donna Carlotta some canary and a sweet cake or some marchpane? I'll leave you to rest, lady, or Martyn will complain that I have wearied you. He should be here soon to assure himself about the condition of his patient."

"This doctor, he has always lived here?"

"Hartington? No he has only recently returned from Cambridge. He will practise medicine in this area. Why do you ask?"

"Something about his voice," she faltered. "It is familiar."

His voice carried a hint of amusement. "You'll not suspect our worthy Martyn of piracy, madam?"

"Of course not."

"He is nothing like you describe. Martyn Hartington is thick-set, dark, almost swarthy of countenance and his sole interest is human anatomy and physic. He is a bore on the subject. I can scarce persuade him to leave his potions and books to hunt with me or seek the play or a bear-baiting."

"Sir, I accuse no one," she sought for words to explain. "The Captain, in his way protected me. The men attempted to harm, rape me, only after he had left the ship. He cannot be held responsible for the accident."

He bent and took her hand, his voice hard. "Had you not been forcibly taken aboard his ship, you would not be blind at this moment. We cannot acquit him of blame, lady."

She nodded weakly as he took a courteous leave of her.

The doctor came just before noon. He pronounced himself satisfied with her and she pleaded to be allowed to rise from her bed.

"Certainly." His manner was brisk and she almost winced at his professional coolness. "You will be well to go below stairs whenever possible and get the air while the weather is good."

She read his thoughts. It was more than likely that she would never again regain her sight. The sooner she became accustomed to her blindness the better.

She listened intently to his voice as he gave more instructions to Martha. Surely she had been mistaken. She had not heard him before. All English voices tended to make her heart pound with sudden terror. This man's voice was decidedly deeper than that of her host, and this had given rise to her doubts, but strive as she might she could detect no likeness to the tones of any man she had heard on *The Kestrel*. Indeed how could there be, when Sir Robin himself had told her that Martyn Hartington had only recently returned from Cambridge.

She could not rid herself of the disquieting thought that the man disliked her, wished she was not forced to be given hospitality at Priors Mallory. It was not his place to comment on her presence here but she wondered if he discussed her with Sir Robin. He took his leave of her courteously and she lay back frowning. He was Sir Robin's dear friend. She hoped that she would not prove to be a subject for disputation between them.

When Martha returned Carlotta reached out and tried to trace the woman's features with her fingertips.

"What do you look like, Martha? Sir Robin, is he handsome or plain? Tell me."

"You can feel my wrinkles for yourself. I'm an old woman, nearly sixty, much too fat for my height. My hair's abundant for all that it's as white as Sir Robin's best ruff I starch for him for a Sunday."

"You're not fat. I do not believe it. I do not hear you wheeze or pant."

"Well, let that be, I must cut down my weight soon, I think."

"And, Sir Robin?"

"There's some as would say he's a handsome man. He's brave yellow hair, straight and fine, blue eyes. He strains them overmuch with reading and they're his best feature as I keep telling him."

"Is he bearded?"

"No. He's not aped that court fashion yet awhile, though I don't doubt it will come."

"And his figure? He seemed strong when he carried me up these stairs."

"Oh, he's strong enough, though tall and stooped with so much writing at his desk. Like a maypole he is, needs to eat more good English beef."

"He studies, you say?"

Martha sighed. "Aye, he does little else, crazed about Latin and Greek verse, poetry and music. Since he was at Cambridge with Master Martyn he's seemed to consider little else, except the house, of course. He'll spend hours with the architect from Lynn planning extensions to the East wing and extending the garden. He plans a bowling green next."

She chattered on and Carlotta listened eagerly. Never before had the words of another meant so much to her. From her lips, she saw the world around her. Since, for the present, Priors Mallory was her world, it was important she should know it thoroughly.

✿ Eight

DURING THE next few days Carlotta found herself exploring her surroundings with a quiet determination. Once over the first terrible shock of her predicament she had earnestly tried to come to terms with her disability. There were times when that seemed totally impossible. She seemed trapped in an impenetrable dungeon of darkness where all communication from outside seemed unreal or deliberately misleading. She relied on Martha for all creature comforts and for her motherly sympathy and understanding, as she came to depend on Sir Robin Mallory for all the knowledge of the world without Priors Mallory and the release his learning and music gave her, from the prison of herself.

He would spend hours reading to her or playing on the lute and virginals and at first he carried her each day below stairs. Later, clinging tightly either to his arm or to Martha's, she managed to make her own way into the dining hall or parlour or into the courtyard, where she would sit for hours strumming at the lute or listening to the faint cooing of the doves in the dovecote. The dogs courted her favour. Her mouth would curve into a smile of real pleasure when she felt the gentle clawing of the bitch, Patch, or the sudden heavy weight of Kendall on her feet. They offered companionship when no human could spare time, or when her own bitterness of spirit craved seclusion from her own kind.

Despite the bad times, which were frequent enough, she summoned up courage to face the future and set about using the senses left to her to establish location. Her hearing became more acute, far quicker than she could have deemed possible, so did her sense of smell and also a strange uncanny awareness she could not explain even to herself. Even before she heard a voice or footsteps she was often conscious that friend or stranger was nearby.

Movement was slow and frightening. Grimly she forced herself to learn the position of every article of furniture in her bed-chamber and the servants were forbidden to remove or misplace anything. The downstairs rooms were more difficult and here she must be escorted to and from table and chair by either Sir Robin or a servant. Eating was an embarrassment. At first Carlotta was forced to submit to being fed by Martha like a child but, at length, provided food was cut for her and the new fork placed at her disposal, she was able to feed herself, not without making some mess in the process. On occasions when guests were present, for Martyn Hartington continued to visit Priors Mallory, she insisted on dining in the privacy of her own room.

The young doctor when attending her professionally expressed himself pleased with her progress.

During the following weeks time seemed to have little reality for Carlotta. She was engaged in the constant struggle to overcome her difficulties and protected in a warm cocoon of care spun for her by Sir Robin, Martha, Hartington and all at Priors Mallory. They seemed anxious for her to forget the outside world and the painful memories it invoked and she was glad for it to be so.

Such an interlude could not, however, last indefinitely and Sir Robin came into the courtyard one day where she sat with the dogs. She detected the concern in his voice and turned her head hurriedly in his direction.

"Did you say there is news for me? What is it? Is there tidings of Sir William?"

"None at all, I regret to say. It will be some time yet before he manages to take passage from the Netherlands. The war has intensified and it may be difficult. No, this letter is from Lady Styles at Buckleigh. She intends to come to you here. Since the length of time that this was written I imagine she cannot be far behind on the road. Her messenger has taken an unconscionable time reaching us."

"Does she know that—that I am blind?"

"No."

"You did not warn her?" She sounded shocked and he sat down beside her on the wooden bench, bending to pull Kendall's ears gently.

"I thought it best not. I had hoped that you would recover. I told her of the attack on the ship and her own husband's plight and that you might need her protection."

"Do you know her?" Carlotta's anxiety was apparent in the softness of the question. "What sort of lady is she—kind?"

"I would not term Lady Anne, kind. She was an heiress and brought Styles considerable wealth. I have met the lady only once that I can recall. She is large."

"Large—you mean tall?"

"I mean large in every way, tall, broad and loud voiced."

"Ill tempered?"

"What we in English call curst—a shrew."

"I know the term. She will not like me."

He shrugged. She almost felt the movement. "It is not for her to like or dislike. She admits your claim on her and she says that since you are hurt she will come herself instead of dispatching servants to escort you to Buckleigh."

"To Buckleigh?" Her voice tailed off uncertainly. "Oh, I had not thought. Of course, I cannot stay here. I trespass—is that the word—on your hospitality."

His voice was grim, as he rose to his feet and put out a hand to help her rise. "I would I could persuade you to accept my hospitality for longer, but we must wait and see what my lady has to say when she arrives. Do not fear. If necessary, Martyn Hartington can say you are unfit yet to travel and delay your departure until we hear further from your uncle."

To Carlotta's dismay the next day brought the arrival of Lady Styles. She had scarcely seated herself in the

knot garden with Martha, when they heard the sound
of the dogs' excited barking. Carlotta listened intently.

"Carriage wheels. Could it be Dr. Hartington, Martha?"

"No, he always rides and not at this hour. He promised to dine with Sir Robin this evening."

"Then—it will be—"

"We shall soon know. Stay here, mistress. Do not disturb yourself and I'll find out for myself."

When she heard Sir Robin's voice at the gate, usher-
ing their visitor into the garden, she knew her surmise
had been correct.

"Donna Carlotta, may I present Lady Styles, who has
hastened from Buckleigh the moment she heard of your
plight."

He came to her side as he saw her groping to rise,
embarrassment at the meeting making her more clumsy
than usual.

"I have informed Lady Styles of your blindness."

Her visitor's voice was indeed loud, authoritative, but
high-pitched, betraying a note of petulance which its
owner had sought to hide.

"My dear niece, I am disturbed beyond words to
hear of your condition. Sir Robin's letter had prepared
me to find you in a state of shock, but that the action of
this deplorable pirate should rob you of your sight as
well as your worldly goods completely unnerves me.
The Queen's justices must hear of this. Without doubt
we shall lodge formal complaint. That it should be an
Englishman who has brought us to this!"

Carlotta held out a hesitant hand. "It is so very kind
that you came to me, señora. I have no right to expect—Sir William has been placed in peril, because of
me."

"Nonsense." Lady Anne's reaction was sharp. "Your
father's action was the foolish one. What in God's name
persuaded him to send you to England unwed? How old
are you—sixteen, seventeen?"

"I shall be eighteen in three weeks, lady."

Lady Anne gave a little shriek of annoyance. "Eighteen, unwed and without dower. What shall we do with you? God preserve us from feckless fathers."

Sir Robin came hastily to Carlotta's assistance. "Donna Carlotta had not the right to question her father's dying wish. Since she loved him dearly, it was agonising enough to accept. I am sure she had no desire to leave her native land and in all events, Lady Styles, as I am sure you will admit, recriminations are useless. We must consider Donna Carlotta's future, not her past."

Though the words were spoken respectfully enough they carried an undoubted sting and Carlotta heard Lady Styles give an imperceptible gasp. She recovered her composure quickly. "My child, what am I saying? I have not embraced you."

Carlotta found herself drawn towards an ample bosom in an almost enveloping embrace. The scent of musk met her nostrils and the thick velvet felt rich to the touch, the studs of jewels marked her cheeks and throat with tiny dents. For the first time she considered her own appearance. She had allowed Martha Wagg to dress her each day without questioning her from where the gown was obtained or even its cut or colour. She had known her newly acquired garments and underlinen to be spotlessly clean by their fresh scent and feel, but now that this woman had arrived, apparently clad in the height of fashion, she could not help worrying as to whether she looked dowdy or ill-clad. Presumably her gowns had belonged, like her night apparel, to Sir Robin's dead mother—and if so, were sadly behind the current mode worn at court or even among wealthy dames in the provinces. Somehow it had never occurred to her, after that first time on the bench, to even mention her appearance to Sir Robin. Other matters had filled her mind. Now, she was suddenly distressed by her own lack of knowledge. Was her hair dishevelled or well-arranged? Martha brushed it lovingly each night and dressed it during the day, but Martha was no lady's maid and perhaps her notions of propriety fell sadly behind the standards set by Lady Styles.

Her uncle's wife was speaking, commanding attention.

"You make me aware of my duty, Sir Robin. Donna Carlotta must return with me to Buckleigh. Sir William would wish it. Poor child, she must not suffer from her father's ill-judgement. Thank God, she is not ill-favoured. Despite the problems which face us, we might still have her wed before the year is out."

Sir Robin held tightly to the little hand which caught at his convulsively.

"May I offer the hospitality of Priors Mallory, Lady Styles, at least until we hear of Sir William's arrival in England."

"Lord bless you, man, no. I'll stay tonight if you'll have me. Tomorrow we'll set out for Northamptonshire. I take it you are fit to travel, niece, you look piquey but strong enough."

"We will consult our physician tonight," Sir Robin said suavely. "My housekeeper will put rooms at your disposal, my lady. I hope you will find all for your pleasure. We live quietly at Priors Mallory but comfortably."

"If first impressions are to be judged, very comfortably. You are enlarging the outbuildings I see. Though there is much to be done, the house seems tolerable enough. How old is it? Did it, as its name suggests, begin life as an Abbey?"

"It was part of the Prior's house, but badly damaged when the religious house was dismantled during King Harry's reforms of our church. The property was given to my father for some service. Our house had fallen into disrepair since 1485. My great-grandfather left England in that year and never returned. We were glad to re-build on the old guest house, as you see. Please come in. Donna Carlotta, will you come with us or wait here for Martha?"

"I will wait, My Lady," Carlotta turned towards the direction in which she hoped her visitor stood. "I will see you after dinner. I do not eat in company. You will understand."

"I see." Lady Styles undoubtedly had not considered. She digested the fact and as graciously as she could bade farewell to Carlotta, promising to present herself to her husband's niece later, in her bed-chamber.

When they had gone Carlotta sank on to the wooden bench and covered her face with her hands. In vain she struggled with her tears and was distressed to find her fingers gently but masterfully withdrawn.

"Donna Carlotta, I had come to expect greater courage from my patient."

Carlotta drew her breath in a gulp. "Dr. Hartington, it is you? I regret I am not usually so foolish."

"Indeed you are not. What is the cause of these tears?"

"Lady Styles has arrived."

"Yes?"

She smiled at the single word, coolly uttered. "She reminds me that I cannot any longer stay hidden here. I must face the world and she seems ill pleased to be burdened with me."

"And she had the ill grace to say so?"

"I am afraid so."

He made no further comment. "I think it wiser if we return to the house."

Carlotta took a solitary meal in her room, as she had requested. Martha served her and, noting her mood of restraint, respected her need for quiet and asked no questions, neither did she comment on the person of Lady Styles. Sir Robin did not come above stairs. Martyn Hartington was admitted by Martha when he knocked after dinner and waited until Martha withdrew to the window-seat.

"You are recovered? Would you wish me to prescribe some posset so that you might sleep?"

"Oh, doctor, of course I do not need such a medicine. I told you I was but foolish in the garden. You did not alarm Sir Robin?"

"I think it unnecessary to inform Sir Robin that you have no wish to accompany Lady Styles to Buckleigh.

Unfortunately I cannot state that you are unfit to leave us. She seems determined to have her way."

"She is a—how do you say—'managing' woman."

"She is," he confirmed and she suspected that his usually stern face relaxed into a grin by the rueful note of his voice. "God help poor Sir William."

"I confess I thought the man a drunken sot until he proved himself more courageous when we were boarded."

"Who would not drown his sorrows in sack who had My Lady to contend with?"

"Doctor, we are unkind?"

"Are we?" She heard him chuckle. "Perhaps you are right. I must leave you with Martha. Alas, the dragon has declared her intention of visiting you and I cannot forbid it. I will leave a draught for you with Martha. No argument. You will take it if you fail to sleep later. You will need your strength if indeed you are to begin your journey tomorrow."

He cursed as he heard a peremptory knock on the door. He nodded to Martha to admit the visitor.

"Well, doctor, how does the patient? She may leave tomorrow?"

He bowed. "If Donna Carlotta considers herself well enough, certainly. She has been an excellent patient. I wish you good health, lady, and better fortune."

She felt his respectful kiss on her hand as he took his leave.

Lady Styles wasted no time on polite preliminaries.

"Very well, woman, you may leave me with your mistress."

Martha hedged. "If Donna Carlotta wishes—"

"Go, woman, I wish to have private words with my niece. You have done your work well. I congratulate you on your care of this lady. Now, off to the servants' hall with you."

Carlotta had already undressed and retired to bed. She was suddenly angry at this woman's dismissal of her companion. She suspected that Martha Wagg was seldom spoken to in so condescending a manner, but she could find no reason to argue with Lady Styles or to recall the housekeeper. Quietly she thanked Martha for her services while two hectic spots of colour burned in her cheeks. Martha withdrew and Carlotta heard the door close softly behind her.

The swish of Lady Styles's skirts told her the woman had drawn close to the bed.

"Now, niece, it is time we became better acquainted." She bent over the bed and Carlotta withdrew, puzzled as she felt faint heat and heard the hiss of a burning candle held close.

"Don't fear. I've a mind to look at you. As I said before, you're not ill-favoured or too Spanish looking. Thank the good God."

Carlotta's lips parted in fury but the woman rushed on.

"Now, miss, tell me truly. How were you misused?"

"Misused—I do not understand?"

"Come, miss, you speak English well enough when it suits you. I noticed that earlier. How were you treated—on the ship?"

"I was not injured. At least—the accident I cannot recall."

"Where were you held?"

"I beg pardon."

Lady Styles made an impatient sound. "Were you kept in the Captain's cabin?"

"Yes."

"I feared as much."

"He did me no harm."

"Indeed."

"I was not to his taste. Like you, señora, he appeared to have a distaste for Spanish blood."

"Who's to wonder at it? Still—I would hardly have thought—" She broke off, biting back further considerations. "You look virginal enough. There's men who will believe you, God a' mercy."

"Lady Styles, my father did not send me to England to barter for a husband."

"Why did he send you, miss?"

"I—I do not know. He believed I would be happier among my mother's people. I am beginning to doubt it."

"Don't snap at me, girl. We'll have to live together, you and I, and I never dissemble."

"Not even in courtesy?"

"God a' mercy, girl, what's the point of courtesy among friends and relations? Plain speaking is what's needed. You're a pretty girl, which is why I thought—well, no matter, we've said enough of that. I doubt it's as you say, best not to pry. That woman dressed you well. We'll not ask where Sir Robin got such gowns and his mother long enough dead."

She rose and opened a door, presumably to the closet where Martha stowed her gowns. "You've several fine ones. We must ask to take them. You cannot travel without clothes."

Carlotta caught at the bed linen in sudden distress. "I owe Sir Robin much. I cannot repay—"

"We'll offer, though God knows where I'll find the money if ransom is demanded for your uncle. I told him he was off on a fool's errand but when did he ever listen to me? You'll find Buckleigh quiet, not as fine as this house. Sir Robin has filled the place with new-fangled panelling, musical instruments and the like and books—enough to stock a university library. None of these at Buckleigh but you'll find the neighbouring squires pleasant enough and tolerant. You're of the old faith, I take it?"

Carlotta coloured. "I am a faithful Catholic."

Lady Styles gave a heavy sigh. "I'd feared it. Then keep the matter quiet. We pay your church fine and no one will know of it. Now I'll leave you." She yawned, "I'm overweary myself and we've a hard task tomorrow. I wonder if Sir Robin would lend us your maid. I'll ask him. You'll need more help than I can give, for a while at least."

She gave a hasty peck at Carlotta's cheek and bustled from the room.

Carlotta sat stock-still against the pillows, her cheeks burning. She knotted and unknotted the sheet in her an-

ger and shame. Lady Styles made her feel an encum-
brance, and not only that an expensive one. How could
she contrive to live with such a woman? She could not
remain a burden on Sir Robin Mallory's charity and
could she repay him now for his care of her? It seemed
unlikely that Lady Styles would attempt to do so. She
choked back further tears as Martha came quietly to
her side with a tankard of mulled ale. She had allowed
herself to behave foolishly too much today. She was no
child but Donna Carlotta Elizabetta de Rodruigez y
Cordoba and she determined that from tomorrow Lady
Anne Styles should not be allowed to forget it.

✎ Nine

CARLOTTA ROSE early, determined that she would not
keep Lady Styles waiting, and her toilet was, of necessity, a lengthy business. Martha grumbled and scolded at
the undue haste but was somewhat mollified to discover
that she was to accompany Carlotta.

"Though how my poor Robin is to manage without
me, the dear Lord knows," she moaned.

She persuaded Carlotta to eat a hearty breakfast
though she had little stomach for it. Afterwards Carlotta
descended the broad newel stair, clinging tightly to
Martha's arm and feeling each tread as she went. No
longer now must she rely on the good offices of Sir
Robin Mallory.

"Take me to him, Martha," she said quietly. "I
would say my good-byes before I see Lady Styles today."

"He's still at breakfast, like as not, since he was up

almost before dawn to attend to the details of your journey."

"I am too much in his debt already."

Martha led her into the dining hall and Carlotta heard Sir Robin's chair scrape back as he rose.

"So, you are almost ready to leave."

"I am, sir, but first I must attempt to thank you, not only for your care of me, but the expense I have caused you."

"Lady, it is of no account."

"Indeed it is. If—" she hesitated, "if aught of my dowry is recovered, you shall be paid in full, sir."

"We shall see." He took her hand and led her to the window seat. She could feel the coolness of the breeze fan her cheek. "You are not too distressed to accompany My Lady?"

"I have no choice, Sir Robin."

"It seems not, however—" he broke off then resumed hurriedly, "life will be easier when Sir William returns and I shall make it my business to know how you fare."

"But how, sir?"

He chuckled lightly. "I have my ways." He paused as if listening and she strained her ears to catch what he sought.

"Horses' hooves? Dr. Hartington?"

"Possibly, but I think not. Excuse me, lady, for one moment for I think your deliverance is at hand."

"My deliverance?" Mystified she put out a hand to stay him but already she heard his quick steps on the flagstones of the hallway. Martha crossed to her side and peered through the open window.

"Two riders. I know them not. One carries a message for Sir Robin."

"Look again, Martha. What is it?"

The old woman craned her head further but declared herself as puzzled as her mistress.

"Donna Carlotta," Sir Robin called joyously as he reentered. "Now we shall see if it is as I hope. She would not fail me, I knew it."

"She? Of whom do you speak, Sir Robin?"

"Why of Bess of course, of the Queen."

"The Queen? You jest, Sir Robin. You have messages from the Queen. It cannot be so."

"Aye, lady, from the Queen and summoning you to Court instantly."

"To Court, Sir Robin?" Carlotta heard Lady Styles's infuriated tones from the doorway. "You say the Queen asks for Donna Carlotta? Why so?"

"Why, madam, how can I know the Queen's intent, but if I heard rightly it was Donna Carlotta's father's wish that she might attend the Queen as once her mother did. She writes in a high rage that any should attack the King of Spain's representative. She is distressed beyond measure at your plight and demands that I bring you before her to lay charges against the culprits. Your evidence is essential if the criminals are to be brought to justice."

"Then we are to go to Court, sir?" Lady Styles, for once, was over-awed.

Sir Robin coughed delicately. "Alas, lady, the Queen makes no mention of you or even Sir William."

"Do you tell me I cannot accompany my niece?"

"There would be naught to prevent you from taking lodgings in London, madam, if you so desire, but would it not be wiser to return to Buckleigh where doubtless some communication from Sir William awaits you? I am sure that later the Queen will wish to hear the story from his lips and indeed he may need your attention."

"But Donna Carlotta?"

"I am commanded to attend Donna Carlotta."

"She cannot go such a journey without chaperone."

"But Martha accompanies us, naturally."

Carlotta remained silent during this duel of wills. She clung tightly to Martha's fingers, content to allow Sir Robin to do battle for her.

"Should Donna Carlotta become ill. The rigours of the journey—?"

"Are no greater than to Northamptonshire. Dr. Hartington has business in the city. I think I can persuade him to go with us earlier than he had planned. We will, of course, inform you of our safe arrival."

His reasoning was so sure that Lady Styles could only swallow her frustration and give a brief nod of acceptance.

"It seems that I must obey the Queen and give Donna Carlotta into your care, if she is satisfied with the arrangement." Her tone implied hope but it was destined to be dashed.

"Lady Styles, I thank you for your concern but since the Queen has interested herself in my affairs, I am sure it would be simpler for you to await Sir William in Buckleigh. He may ride straight to you and be anxious or if his messenger finds you not at home it may delay his plans. You yourself said you had no notion how you were to meet the extra expense of my charge on you. Now it seems that you will be spared it. Should the Queen not require my services, which I feel she cannot under the circumstances, the Spanish Ambassador will make himself responsible for my safety. I shall return to my relatives in Spain."

Lady Styles gave a little sigh. "Then it appears I am no longer needed and can take my journey to Buckleigh this morning, as I planned, but alone. When will you travel, Sir Robin?"

"We shall set forth later today. The Queen requires there shall be no delay, and, fortunately, Donna Carlotta is attired and packed for a journey."

Carlotta returned Lady Styles's kiss of farewell more warmly than she could have thought possible. She was so delighted to have that lady leave without her, she would have been even more gracious had she not been so excited and disturbed by her own impending departure. Sir Robin went out to see Lady Styles leave and to ensure her safe journey supplied two sturdy men of his own to go with her to Buckleigh. Carlotta waited for his return.

"You are a magician, Sir Robin," she said gaily when he came back to her. "It is true—we are to journey to London?"

"We cannot disobey our glorious Bess."

"I—had not thought at first—but now—I am afraid."

"To face the Queen?"

"She can have no love for Spaniards."

"If she has none she has strange ways of showing her hatred. She wooes the Spanish Ambassador as a village swain his sweetheart. Give yourself no qualms, lady, Bess will receive you well. She speaks warmly of remembrances of your mother."

"Is she not shrewish, like Lady Styles?"

He laughed. "Aye, that she can be, and more so. She can swear like a Billingsgate fishwife or any whore from the stews of Bankside and when it suits her, she can coo as sweetly as a dove from yonder dove-cote. She is all things to all men."

"And to women?"

"Ah, that I'll not say. She'll find no fault with your looks. Even your hair is of her own colour, though darker of hue. She can be jealous, our Bess, but wondrous gentle, and I've no doubts of her sympathy for you."

"You appear to know her well, sir."

"I've been to Court and seen my fill of it. My family has not been received well at Court until lately, when the Queen, with her usual contrariness, saw fit to look on me with favour. She likes my wit, she says. I amuse her with my verses and my music.

"Why was your father out of favour? I do not understand."

"It is a long story. You are acquainted with English history?"

"My father saw that I understood in general terms."

"You must know then that the Tudor King Henry, our Queen's grandfather, defeated our sovereign Lord King Richard at Bosworth."

"You speak of this dead King with respect. Did I not hear that he himself was both usurper and murderer?"

"Did you so?" His voice was gentle but betrayed a note of hard steel.

"It was not so?"

"That, lady, I will not dispute with you. My family was ever true to York. My grandfather fought and bled at Bosworth, aye, and later too, at Stoke. It was the only time he returned to England from Burgundy after 1485. We are of the old allegiance and we stay true. My father returned at young King Harry's request and for some reason was later granted this land."

"Yet you worship at this Tudor Queen's Court."

"Aye." His voice was tender. "She bears Plantagenet blood, our Bess, and for that I'll serve her, if her claim is hardly just. Without her England has no hope. There are no heirs of Richard's blood worthy to contend with her. There, enough, I rarely talk politics. It is not wise."

"If your family was not fairly pledged to the Tudor, are you of the old faith?"

"No. Most of us are—we who served the House of York, but I have heard so much that sickened me of cruelty and death during the old Queen's reign and of the Inquisition that I worship my God in the new way. Like our Queen I am tolerant. Provided you are circumspect no one will dispute with you on this matter if you refrain from services."

She was silent for some moments then she said, "I too have seen much that horrified me, not in Spain. From autos and such sights I was protected—but on the English ship—those men, treated like animals. I think my father knew that I would fall under suspicion in my own land, since, unlike my friends, I question my faith. I believe it was for this he sent me from Spain, yet despite the hatred and the wilful misreading of God's Holy word by corrupt priests and bigots, I cannot but hold to my own faith."

"And no one will seek to turn you from it. Certainly not I."

Martha had left to attend to the disposal of the baggage. Now she called that Dr. Hartington had arrived. Sir Robin took Carlotta's hand.

"Come, let me help you to the carriage."

"You are ready, so soon?"

He laughed. "I had already prepared for this. Had

the Queen not summoned you, I had intended to ride to London."

"For what reason?"

His answer sounded faintly amused. "Why—to put your case before her, surely."

Martha made Carlotta comfortable in the carriage and sat opposite chattering brightly to dispel the boredom of the journey. Carlotta could not put aside the thought that this, her first experience of travel in England, would have delighted her if only she had been able to see the countryside. Now she was forced to sit in the close darkness of the carriage, and she was soon conscious of a feeling of overwhelming sickness. Resolutely she thrust it aside and attempted to concentrate on Martha's chatter. She had never been a poor traveller and when poor Teresa had been forced to seek her bunk in the cabin during the voyage Carlotta had not once been troubled. She put up a hand to her brow and drew it away wet with perspiration. The carriage wheels bumped and clattered over the ruts in the road since the weather had been dry during the last weeks and their increased clamour seemed to add to her distress. She felt that she could scarce breathe. She swallowed hard, but the threat of sickness returned with increasing force and she gave a little cry.

"Martha, please, ask Sir Robin to stop the carriage."

Martha leant forward worriedly. "What is it, chicken? Are you unwell?" She dashed aside the leathern curtain and called to the coachman to pull up.

Sir Robin galloped back to the carriage and drew rein alongside as Martyn Hartington joined him.

"What is it?" The doctor's voice was anxious.

Martha helped Carlotta alight and she retched miserably at the roadside. Hartington dismounted, unstrapped a bag from his saddle bow and hurried towards her. He gestured Martha aside and offered a towel dampened with rosewater.

"Wipe your face, Donna Carlotta. Sit on the carriage step for a while. This will soon pass."

He went back to his horse and withdrew a small phial

from his bag. Sir Robin had also dismounted and was regarding Donna Carlotta, frowningly. He detained the doctor as he was about to rejoin his patient.

"What is wrong? Is she—"

The other laughed. "No, certainly not. Give your heart peace. I expected this. She has not yet recovered from the accident and the noise of the carriage in her darkness is distressing."

Carlotta took the phial from him. He pulled out the stopper and guided her hand close to her nostrils.

"Gently, now. Inhale. You will feel better."

She gave a little gasp, then a cough, then said tremulously, "I am so sorry, I felt—that I could not breathe and so sick." She shuddered.

"I fear the movement of the carriage is upsetting you. We must go more slowly," Hartington said quietly.

"But I have never before suffered so."

"Your blindness increases the feeling of suffocation. Try to relax."

She nodded. "Yes, that is exactly how I feel, but we must not delay if the Queen commands."

"That need not disturb you," Sir Robin interposed. "Her Grace will understand, but," he turned to Hartington, "you say, you think it is the carriage?"

"I am sure of it."

"Then, lady, you must ride."

"Ride?" Martha gave a cry of dismay. "Impossible, sir. Donna Carlotta could not—"

"Sit a horse unaided." He finished for her. "Of course not." He leaned down and took Carlotta's hand. "Better?"

She gave a strangled laugh. "Yes, sir, I thank you."

"Then you will ride pillion like a farmer's wife to market. How say you, lady, to sit behind me?"

She gave a startled cry, half sob. "But, sir—"

"What would people say?" Martha rounded on him angrily.

He shrugged lightly. "I care not what people say, and I doubt if Donna Carlotta does, but if it disturbs you, Martha, why, we'll take to the carriage again when we near the towns. How say you, Donna Carlotta, will you trust yourself to me?" He waited, eyebrow raised comically for her reply.

She hesitated but only for a moment. Now that she had emerged from the stifling carriage and could feel the sun on her face and the breeze fan her cheeks she longed to do as he suggested, however outrageous it appeared. "Yes," she said quickly, "oh yes, please, let me sit a horse out in the open. I am not used to vehicles."

He regarded her critically. "You have no habit. Martha," he said at last, "take my lady back to the carriage and remove that monstrous hoop."

Martha gave a second wail of dismay which he silenced with one wave of his hand.

"Come, would you have me become tire-woman? Do as I say. We do what is best for Donna Carlotta, not what is good for propriety."

When Dr. Hartington lifted her to Sir Robin's saddle she felt a joyous thrill at the familiar feel and smell of her mount.

"Clasp me tightly," Sir Robin exhorted her cheerfully and she obeyed with alacrity, then they were off once more.

It hardly seemed possible she could have enjoyed the journey so much. Exhilaration of movement brought the colour to her cheeks and she laughed aloud as he set his mount to a light canter and she sensed his nearness, giving her confidence and a feeling of security she had never known. So many times she had relied on his sturdy strength to carry or lead her, now she thrilled to the ripple of his muscles under her hands and as he shouted to warn her of greater speed she but laughed more loudly.

About four of the afternoon Sir Robin dismounted near Littleport and while a groom held his horse still, lifted Carlotta gently to the ground. Martha hurried forward, the light of battle in her eyes to set to rights the appearance of her charge, but Carlotta was content to sit beside them on the green sward and eat cold meats and venison pasty, taking a delight in the simple fare.

Afterwards Martyn Hartington spurred ahead with the groom to seek the best accommodation the little town could offer. Martha drew aside to discuss the baggage with the coach-driver.

"Am I greatly dishevelled?" Carlotta put up a searching hand to her hair, piled up high only this morning by Martha's deft fingers.

"You look exquisite. Diana, the huntress goddess."

"Do not tease me, sir."

"Shall I not?" His voice dropped and she leaned forward slightly, detecting a new note in his raillery, then drawing back in some confusion.

He rattled on, some nonsense of verse to her beauty, but she was not listening so intently. Her heart was beating still more quickly than she had known. At first she had put the phenomenon down to the vigour of the ride, now she was not so sure. She had come to know this man so well, to need him. What was their relationship? She would have been a fool to have been unaware of his growing affection—dare she term it love? Did he pity her, this gay, clever, learned Englishman or did he desire her truly? And what did she feel for him—completely safe in his presence, contented, as happy as her affliction would allow. When he was not close, then her world was indeed in blackness; with him close by, she could detect some ray of light, of hope, of yearning. At Priors Mallory she had learned to live with this terrible shadow of darkness and fear. Had love given her this courage, and if it had, what wife could she be to him? Always she would need to be led, guided, carefully nurtured, no careful chatelaine of his lovely home as he had hoped the woman of his choice would be. Worst of all she brought no dower to soften the difficulties of his burden. It could not be, yet, for the present, while he was here, completely at her service, as he was now, she could rejoice in his nearness.

Inns in Littleport did not accommodate more than two people so Martha slept soundly on the floor of Carlotta's tiny room though Carlotta protested sharply. Dr. Hartington went with the driver, groom and the coach to another inn some two miles outside the town and Sir Robin quietly settled himself in the inn parlour. The anxious innkeeper made him as comfortable as possible on the huge oak settle with pillows and a blanket.

Sir Robin laughed at Carlotta's objections. "I shall most probably be the more excellently lodged. Though Martyn has viewed your chamber, I am not entirely sat-isfied that the fleas from the mattress will not bite in the night. Sleep in your clothing and rest on my cloak."

Carlotta was too wearied to find any fault in her lodging and after climbing awkwardly up the rickety wooden stair, preceded by the innkeeper's wife, whose concern was almost comical, and Martha, instructing from behind, she threw herself almost fully clothed, as Sir Robin had suggested, on to the crude wooden frame bed and found its thongs and down and straw mattress well enough. She slept dreamlessly and woke thoroughly refreshed to wash hurriedly and go below to eat a hearty breakfast of cold meats, ale, rye bread and honey in the inn-parlour with Sir Robin. This morning Martha had dressed her simply so that she might ride with Sir Robin since the day was fine. Hartington joined them later and complimented his patient.

"That green velvet becomes you, Donna Carlotta, and you look well."

"I feel excellently refreshed, Doctor."

The journey to the university city was uneventful and Sir Robin regaled her with sundry tales of his activities when he had proved a lawless student at Kings. Since the city was of some size and importance Carlotta con-sented to be returned to the carriage for the last few miles of the journey and found that the sickness which had troubled her yesterday did not reappear. Martha fussed over her appearance and it was an excellently groomed Carlotta who entered the parlour of the 'Three Tuns' on the arm of Sir Robin. The groom had already spurred ahead and accommodation was bespoken for all but Martyn Hartington who had accepted an invitation from an old student companion to dine with him when-ever he found himself in the city and he declined to eat with them, assuring them that if he did not return that night he would be ready to begin their journey with them in the morning.

Supper was taken in a private chamber and was excellent. Carlotta was not so wearied tonight and when she heard a sudden commotion in the courtyard outside she leaned towards her companion enquiringly.

He rose and went to the casement.

"A company of strolling players. They seem a poor enough company, but they'll draw a crowd right enough."

"Players, actors?" Carlotta drew a sudden breath of pure excitement. She had heard of such groups which travelled the length and breadth of the country trundling their few costumes and properties on a cart pulled by some patient donkey, but had never before had an opportunity of seeing them perform.

He turned, amusement apparent in his voice, "You would wish to hear them?"

"Oh could we, please?"

"Why not, if you are not too wearied. I'll obtain stools for us. Martha?" He appealed to his housekeeper.

"If you please, sir, you'll excuse me. I'm tired and I'd prefer to go to our chamber and prepare Donna Carlotta's clothes for tomorrow. I've not heart for such fripperies."

He laughed again. "Certainly, Martha, do as you please. Check my sheets are aired, there's a good woman."

Later Carlotta sat in the courtyard clinging tightly to his hand as the motley crowd swarmed by them. Boos and catcalls from an exuberant group of students greeted the appearance of the prologue who addressed the audience in loud and ringing tones.

Sir Robin explained in a whisper. "They are to perform a version of 'The Trojan Women'. You will know the tale?" As she nodded he continued, "All the parts of the women will be played by young boy apprentices. Mark the shrillness of their accents. The clothing is of poor quality but effective." He chuckled, "The King,

Priam, wears a monstrous crown and his jewelled chain is fine enough to deck the Earl of Leicester, himself. Queen Hecuba is overpainted, I fear, and somewhat rounded, if what I imagine of that most unfortunate of Queens is true, but the boy speaks his lines well enough."

The play proceeded ably. If it had faults in the performance, Carlotta did not note them. She sat entranced listening intently, and so indeed did the crowd which thronged the courtyard. She found herself weeping for the luckless Andromache and the tragic Cassandra and when the play ended and a rousing cheer rose from the packed assembly in the courtyard, she came to herself with a sudden start.

"You are safe enough, here for a moment?" Sir Robin handed her his lawn kerchief and she ruefully dabbed at her eyes. "Soon the apprentice lads will be round for the reckoning. Give them the contents of this purse. I will return in a moment. I wish to speak with one of the company. I've seen the man before and would give him a word of worldly advice."

She nodded happily and felt him move away. No one sought to accost her. It was clear enough by her dress she was under the protection of the gentlemen who accompanied her and she was left to sit quietly, reflecting on the play. A jingle of coins and one or two ribald phrases caught her ear. Good-humouredly the boy collectors were twitted, as each member of the audience reluctantly parted with silver groats and copper coins.

As the velvet hat was placed under her hand Carlotta fumbled with the fastening of the mesh purse Sir Robin had left with her. "Wait, boy, one moment."

She paused as a hasty whisper cut across the noise and confusion around her, yet carried clearly enough.

"Donna Carlotta, lady, thank God I have found you again. I sought you for hours."

The coins tumbled unheeded from the purse, some into the velvet bonnet to join those previously collected, others to fall to the ground and cause a sudden scuffle round her feet.

"Peter?" her answering whisper was uncertain and incredulous.

"Yes it is I. Do you not know me, lady?"

"Peter, where are you? I cannot see, boy, I am blind. You are well—not harmed by those men?"

"Blind?" His bewilderment was as great as hers. "Yes, I am unharmed. They left me unconscious and there was no sign of you on the quay. I dared not enquire too closely. Lady, I must speak with you—" He broke off sharply as Sir Robin pushed his way firmly but pleasantly through the gathering.

"Peter," she gave an alarmed cry as she felt the boy slip by her clinging fingers and dash off into the crowd. Sir Robin's velvet-clad sleeve was all that her searching fingers found and he questioned her worriedly.

"What is it? Did the boy steal from you? Shall I follow?"

"Robin, did you see him—that boy?"

"No, at least not well. As I approached he flew off."

"He was the boy I told you about, the boy from the ship who helped me escape."

"But I thought he was one of the boy actors."

She broke in impatiently. "I don't know. I think he was collecting the coins for the players. He tried to say something to me but then you arrived."

"You think I frightened him off, is that it?"

She had the grace to blush for his tone implied blame.

"I—I don't know. Something did. Oh, if only I could see." For the first time for days tears were perilously close to the surface and she blinked them back angrily. "There was so much I wanted to know. If only he had stayed."

"Shall I search for him?"

"No." She bit her lip. "I think he will hide. For some reason he is afraid. He may think I hold him responsible for what happened. At all events he served aboard a pirate vessel and that is a hanging matter if he is caught."

"True enough, but if the boy could be persuaded to

talk, he could give valuable information. What does he look like? If I see a lad answering to his description I'll demand an explanation."

She tried to think, to focus her mind back to the frightening days on board *The Kestrel*.

"It is difficult, just a boy, tall, tousle-haired, fair, I think. I did not note him unduly. He said he had something to say to me."

"I think you should retire. You are overtired and strained and have the journey to face tomorrow."

"Promise you will not drive him away or betray him. In his way he was good to me."

"If the boy presents himself, he will be brought to your side and I will do my utmost to prevent him from paying the price of his former folly."

"Thank you. I am sorry if I was sharp. Pray forgive me, sir. For once my blindness irked me sorely, worse than usual."

He took her cold fingers tight within his own. "Not one of us forgets your outstanding courage, Donna Carlotta. The Queen shall know of it—now, to bed."

Martha grumbled that it was late when she assisted her charge to disrobe and climb into the comfortable lavender-scented bed. This inn certainly boasted more luxuries than the one at Littleport. Carlotta was thankful to rest back and close her eyes. The sudden encounter with the boy, Peter, and his subsequent disappearance had disturbed her and she feared now that she would not sleep. Martha remarked sourly that it was like Sir Robin to put a stupid show before the wellbeing of his charge.

"Do not scold him, Martha. I pleaded to hear the play."

"I'll go down to the parlour and ask that slut of an inn wench to heat you some milk. It will help to lull you off. If Mr. Martyn were here he would give you some posset."

"I'm glad he is not," Carlotta laughed weakly, "or he might have forbidden me to go to the play. Dear Martha, fetch me the milk, for I think it will help me to rest."

She wanted to be alone for while, to think, to concentrate. Peter had sounded excited, anxious to impart news or a warning. Did he know where *The Kestrel* was or the identity of her Captain? The boy had said they left him unconscious of the quay. Then he had not returned to *The Kestrel*. And why was he now working with the play company? Dare he no longer face his former Captain, and, if so, was the boy prepared to betray him?

Someone opened the door. She turned her head towards the betraying sound of the latch clicking.

"Martha, you were quick. I thought you would linger in the kitchen."

The housekeeper made no reply and footsteps approached the bed.

"Martha?" Again Carlotta spoke urgently, anxious to have the identity of her nurse-companion confirmed.

The footsteps quickened and Carlotta heaved herself upright.

Her visitor's breathing quickened but still nothing was said. Surely those were not Martha's steps, light assured. The old woman's were heavier, more laboured.

"Who is it?" Carlotta questioned, now thoroughly alarmed. Who but Martha would come to her chamber now?

"Peter?" She whispered the name. Was that it? Had the boy discovered the position of her chamber and sought her out?

Her outstretched arms reached out and encountered a velvet-clad sleeve. The man's breath was warm on her cheek, wine-fumed. She struggled, opened her lips to call out and felt one hand clamp hard over her mouth. She knew as she fought rising panic that he was not the cabin boy. This man was bigger, stronger, and he meant her harm. She writhed in his hard grasp, twisting this way and that to force him to release his hold; then, terrifyingly, she felt cold steel pressed hard against her breast. In that second of revelation she knew her unknown assailant meant to kill her. Instinctively she did the only thing she could; though it might mean her death, she bit down savagely on the hard hand which held her silent. The dagger tore across her breast and shoulder, surprisingly giving little pain. The man cried out, then chokingly attempted to curtail the sound. He cursed roundly, but momentarily he had freed her. She screamed and screamed and fought her way free from his clutch falling from the bed to become entangled in the sheets and coverlet. Still she screamed and when her lungs failed her, crouched upon the ground sobbing and panting in pain and terror.

Noise on the stairs, a confused shouting. She heard a wrenching pull on the casement, a splintering crash as her door was hurled wide, then people moving around, a girl crying hysterically and strong arms lifting her to the bed. She sobbed and struggled, felt the sticky cloying feel of blood on her fingers, down her night-robe, a voice demanding water, a hand soothing her, pressing back her sweat-drenched hair, then she fell against the strong shoulder and knew no more.

🏵 Ten

CARLOTTA SWAM upwards to consciousness. She could hear people talking in muted tones. She strove to speak, yet knew, ashamed, that all she could do was to cry weakly. Gradually she became aware of pain round the region of her left breast and soreness stretching to the shoulder and down her arm. A cool voice, professional, devoid of concern came to her from across the room.

"The wound is not deep. I've cleansed it thoroughly

but it bled excessively. She tore it further in her fall
from the bed. It will have weakened her, but she should
do well enough when she is rested."

Sir Robin's voice, warmer, lighter, familiar. "She is
badly shocked. How soon before she recovers consciousness?"

"Do not hasten the process. Let nature take its own
time."

Hartington had returned then? Had he been hastily
summoned? How did he come to be in the inn so soon?
Indeed, how long had she been unaware of her surroundings? She was too exhausted to draw attention to
her own wakefulness, and lay back, frowning, as she attempted to recall the terrifying happening in the room.
The man had come in when Martha left her for the
milk. He had meant to kill her, no question of that. A
shudder ran through her frame at the remembrance of
his nearness, his breath on her cheek, and his hard
panted gasps. But why—why did he wish to kill her, to
silence her? Peter had made himself known in the
courtyard. He wanted to tell her something—what? It
was of such importance that her assailant was determined that she should not know it, or, if she did know
it, would not pass on that information to others, to Sir
Robin or Dr. Hartington—

An arm lifted her head. She reached out and clutched
at a velvet-clad sleeve and gave a little scream. The
man with whom she'd struggled was so clad.

Hartington's cool voice reassured her. "Donna Carlotta, can you hear me? There is nothing to fear. It is I,
Martyn Hartington. Drink this. You'll feel better."

She swallowed obediently, but her whole being
shrank from him.

"Martha?" she whispered doubtfully.

"I'm here, chicken." Martha's voice was pain-filled,
indignation at her own neglect apparent in the depth of
her grief. "I'll take the cup, Doctor. Drink, dearest.
Martha will not leave you again."

She put the cup down and the doctor placed Carlotta

back against the pillows. She felt Martha's older, harder hands pull the coverings gently back round her shoulders.

"Sir Robin?" Carlotta pulled herself urgently upwards.

"I'm here, lady. Do as Martha and the doctor said. There's naught to fear."

She clutched at his hand, tears falling faster now. "Please, Sir Robin—the boy, Peter, is he safe?"

He bent his head close to her lips. "What do you say? The boy? There's no boy here."

"No, no," she struggled to explain. "The killer—the man in the room. He will try to kill the boy too."

"She's restless," the doctor said quietly, "a little light-headed. The potion will soon do its work. She must sleep."

Sir Robin must know—must understand. Weakly she appealed, her lips working pitifully.

"Find the boy. Stop the man—"

"Yes, certainly, lady, do not fret. Martha will sleep with you in the bed. You'll be perfectly safe."

"I'll stay outside the door in case of need." Martyn Hartington signalled to Sir Robin.

"No, no," Carlotta forced her drooping lids open. "No, don't let him stay, please—"

Sir Robin's voice was gently remonstrative. "Donna Carlotta, what is this? Do you fear Dr. Hartington?"

"No," her answer was a faint sigh. She swallowed hard. "Forgive me, I trust no one. Let Martha stay, I'll do well enough." She caught once more at Sir Robin's hand. "I'm sorry—"

Unconsciousness was descending again. Vaguely she heard a distant knock on the door and the innkeeper's voice.

"No sign of anyone, sir. The pails were knocked over and the rain water barrel overturned when he jumped from the roof. We're still searching."

Sir Robin's answer was too low for her to catch, then he said, "Dr. Hartington and I will sleep out here in the corridor."

"Aye, sir. I'll bring blankets and pillows."

She heard the door close as he withdrew. She gave a sigh and ceased to fight against the drug. She was safe here with Martha close and the two men outside. Her eyes closed at last and she slept.

Hartington came early to his patient next morning. He put a cool hand on her brow.

"Little fever. How do you feel?"

"Better, but sore."

"Only a flesh wound. It will heal quickly and leave only the smallest of scars. You are fortunate, lady."

"Any news of my attacker?"

"None that I've heard."

Later when Carlotta had breakfasted she told her story to Sir Robin and the doctor. Martha sat gravely by the bedside.

Sir Robin was thoughtful. "I've offered a substantial reward for news of the boy."

"He did not attack me."

"You are sure?"

"Very sure. It was a man, much older, well dressed." She hesitated. "I distinctly felt the velvet of his doublet."

"And believed him to be me?" Hartington said the words unemotionally.

In the morning, safe and secure with her friends about her, the notion seemed ridiculous. Carlotta flushed scarlet.

"I was hysterical, sir. As my doctor, I am sure you will understand and forgive me."

"Certainly." He rose. "I will return to Dr. Arnatt's lodging, Robin. I was so hastily summoned from there last night, that he will be anxious. I'll return this evening to redress the wound and ensure that my patient is comfortable. In the meantime endeavour to keep her quiet."

Martha clattered below for some fruit from the kitchen. Sir Robin was so silent that for a moment Carlotta thought he had gone also and left her alone. When he spoke he startled her so that she jumped.

"Still suspicious? Why did you connect Martyn with the attack?"

"I—I have said. I felt the doublet. They seemed alike."

He considered. "Did you ask Martha for a description of me?"

Her face flamed.

"I see I have my answer."

"No, it isn't what you think."

"No?"

She bit her lip, uncertain how to proceed. "I—I simply wanted to know what you looked like, out of—interest." Her excuse sounded lame even to her own ears. "I could not ask you."

He placed his arm near to her fingers. "Feel."

She drew back as if he had struck her but he insisted. "Feel my sleeve."

She did so reluctantly.

"Velvet, as is Martyn's."

"You make me ashamed."

"No, I am merely puzzled why you will not trust Hartington. You *can* do so, utterly, I assure you. He is entirely at your service. I can vouch for the fact that he was at Dr. Arnatt's lodging when we sent for him."

"Who would wish me dead?"

"Some man of the crew, obviously. The boy attempted to warn you. You told me this yourself. He knew someone here who wished to silence you before you talk before the Queen, some man you can recognise."

"Among the players?"

"Possibly. The boy knew of his nearness and that he would recognise you. It might account for the richness of the cloth. The players were still in costume."

"But I cannot recognise anyone."

"Our assailant is obviously not aware of that fact. He wished either to preserve his own skin or that of his master."

"His master?"

"We must remember that the Captain of *The Kestrel* is our principal criminal. He may be known to the Queen but not in such a role."

"I see." She sank back in the bed. "Then at Court I shall continue to be in danger."

"You must be well guarded. I'll see to that, never fear. Now Martha comes and she will send me away. Try to sleep."

"We shall be delayed."

He patted her hand gently. "I have sent my groom ahead to Greenwich. We cannot travel for some days or your wound will break open again."

She nodded and when Martha returned to sit by her, did as he advised and settled herself to sleep.

Carlotta did not recall much of her final journey to London. They remained at the inn for three days, and she slept most of the time, always conscious that one or other of her faithful watch-dogs kept guard at her side.

There was no news of Peter. He appeared to have vanished as mysteriously as he had come again into her life. She worried about him constantly, fearing that some mischief had happened to the lad, but Martyn Hartington's potions allowed her to slide off into slumber and when he decided that she was fit to travel he insisted that she continue to take the medicine and so she found herself dozing in the carriage for most of the journey, her head resting on Martha's lap. They went slowly, resting at Bishop's Stortford for two days when Carlotta seemed fevered and Hartington forbade any progress until she recovered. At last they clattered into the capital and the noise and rattle and raucous cries about her kept her wakeful. She pushed herself up against the leathern squabs of the coach and thrilled to the sound. They had reached their destination. Soon she must tell her story to the Queen, but her face fell when she realised that with the ending of the journey there must also come an ending to her association with Sir Robin Mallory and Dr. Martyn Hartington, so when

Robin led her slowly into the lodgings he had procured for her close to the Palace of Greenwich, he found her strangely subdued, and was concerned lest her wound was again troubling her.

🍃 *Eleven*

"EXCELLENT." SIR ROBIN crossed the room to stand by Carlotta's side as Martha completed her work and handed her her ostrich ivory-handled fan. "You've done very well indeed, Martha. Now leave us while I explain to Donna Carlotta what will happen."

Martha had minutely described to her the gown Sir Robin chose for her presentation.

It was of white velvet, simple, but well cut. Her far-thingale was wide and in the latest style, her under-robe of white silk, quilted and trimmed with seed pearls as was her tightly styled bodice and stomacher, complete with the immensely wide sleeves. Her neckline was cut low, as became her maiden state and Carlotta could feel for herself the high-boned and starched lace collar which stood out from behind her head and shoulders. Martha had whispered an explanation as she dressed her mahogany-coloured hair high, like the Queen's own, threading a row of small seed pearls to nestle among the richness of colour and texture, one huge pearl falling on to Carlotta's broad high forehead. She had made only one request, that she should wear her father's miniature and she looped its chain anxiously in her fingers and clutched at the handle of her fan as Sir Robin seated himself by her, on the window seat.

"I do not need to tell you how lovely you look. Martha will already have done so, and you may take her word. She has arrayed you splendidly but without ostentation. It is good to honour the Queen in one's best, but not wise to attempt to surpass her, you understand?"

"Very well, sir."

"I shall lead you into her presence and stand by you while you make your courtsey. She knows you will be shy and frightened and will receive you with only her ladies and Sir Francis Walsingham present at this first interview. He is her Secretary of State, intensely interested in all matters pertaining to England and Spain, so it is imperative that he should hear your story at first hand. He is a thin, dark, saturnine man. His questions may be shrewd and sharp. Do not be afraid to answer him frankly. He is kindly and well-meaning and will not embarrass you before Her Grace."

"And the Queen, will she not receive me badly?"

"The Queen wishes you well. She has assured me of her kindly intentions but Bess can be overpowering. She likes flattery but without obsequiousness. Speak up clearly. If you feel faint do not fear to tell me so. Martyn's still concerned that you remain weak after the loss of so much blood. The Queen will understand your need to withdraw."

He reached out and clasped her hand as an indication that he was ready, and she rose in obedience to his guidance.

Despite his reassurance she felt far from convinced that all would be well while they waited in the Queen's private chamber. A page had informed them that the Queen was this moment in Council and would receive them immediately the business under discussion was concluded.

Carlotta felt that her limbs were turning to water and she clumsily let fall her fan, dropping awkwardly to her knees to search for it. Sir Robin cursed softly beneath his breath and stooped to retrieve it for her. It was thus that both were startled by the abrupt opening of a door and turning at the same moment struck their heads one against the other.

"God's teeth, here's an idyll." A loud decisive voice carried to Carlotta, now very close to tears. "Get up, get up, Sir Robin, you've been on your knees before another lady, I see. Bad lad, you've deserted the worship of your sovereign and you promised to be faithful till death."

Robin sounded unabashed as he drew Carlotta to her feet and led her unerringly forward.

"Your Grace delights to torment your humble servants. You know well you are a star too high for my poor grasp. Allow me to present to you Donna Carlotta Elizabetta de Rodruigez y Cordoba."

Carlotta sank into a deep Court curtsey. She had been presented to His Catholic Majesty King Philip on more than one occasion but had never before this moment felt so tongue-tied and afraid.

The Queen's voice bade her briskly to rise. "Come, child, I hear you have not been well. Fetch a stool for her, Sir Robin, but first, give me your hand, come to the light. Let me look well at you."

Carlotta was swept to the window. She felt the slight breeze on her cheek and the wiry grasp of the long slender fingers on her wrist. She felt her chin turned to the light and the Queen said in a soft tone,

"So, little Janet's child. I would not have thought it. She was charming and pretty, but she had none of this beauty of bone structure you have. You are your father's daughter in looks, child, but for your hair." She laughed a pure fluting high laugh of glee. "We were both so carrot-headed, Janet and I. I remember her hair bright against the grey stones of the Tower. Ah, those days bring back laughter and tears. Did she tell you that she requested of the Queen, my sister, that she should go with me to the Tower? Poor dear little Janet. She was terrified every minute of the days we spent there, but she came. I'll not forget that—and now you have come. Well, in good time. Come rest as I bade you. Your gallant squire has done well by you." She spoke to Sir Robin across the room. "You've dressed her finely, sir. You and her maid servant are to be congratulated, but then you've ever had an eye for fine feathers."

"Your Majesty honours me. It has been good to assist Donna Carlotta in her need."

The Queen drew Carlotta back to her chair in the centre of the room. "Sit, child. Your stool is behind you, near the foot of my chair. And you, Sir Robin, sit by the window. Now, I have been hearing strange tales of your journey. You were attacked and hurt. You are better?"

"I am, Your Majesty. The care I have received has hastened my recovery."

"So," the Queen tapped the arm of her chair with her fan. "Tell me what you think inspired this attempt on your life?"

"I cannot tell, Majesty, except that a cabin-boy from the pirate ship *The Kestrel* was present in Cambridge. He saw me and tried to communicate with me. I think my assailant was anxious to prevent us talking further."

"It seems so. Sir Robin, was the boy arrested?"

"Unfortunately not, Your Majesty. We found no sign of him and the assailant made good his escape in our concern for Donna Carlotta's life."

"Yes. Sir Robin, ask my page to summon Sir Francis Walsingham. If Donna Carlotta is not too exhausted, we will hear her story of the attack on *The Isabella* immediately, while the memory is still strong."

Carlotta was glad to be seated while she waited nervously for the Queen's trusted minister to arrive.

Sir Francis greeted her with grave courtesy. He seated himself at the Queen's command and Carlotta told her story as succinctly and directly as she could, without hysterics or emotion.

Sir Francis's questions were careful and gently probing.

"You are certain, without doubt, that *The Kestrel* was an English ship?"

Carlotta gasped at the implication. "Sir, I am convinced. Do you say I was deliberately deceived?"

"I say nothing, Señora, I merely ask that you may inform me more clearly on this matter."

She faltered. "It is possible that it was not. At the time I did not question the fact. The English prisoners were released and treated so kindly—"

"And the other prisoners? There were others. Were they received on board this English ship?"

"I think so."

"You are not sure? You were not conducted round the vessel?"

"I went on deck several times. The crew spoke English."

"And the Captain?"

"He spoke Spanish—to me."

"Fluently?"

"Very fluently."

"You say you saw him clearly, that he was very red-haired and bearded."

"I did not see his hair."

"Why not—was he masked, visored?"

"No, he wore a silk handkerchief—I concluded he was red-haired."

"And he treated you well."

"He offered me no blows nor did he insult me unduly—" She broke off, about to refer to the facial blows she had received and for some reason was unwilling to make this accusation. The thought of it brought the blood to whip her cheeks with unwonted colour.

Sir Francis considered. "Your Majesty, I had word an hour ago that Sir William Styles has landed at Harwich. He brings King Philip's representative, Don Miguel Hernandez. Apparently *The Isabella* reached Dunkirk safely though not without incident. The Spanish hidalgo will naturally be incensed at the seizure of his personal gold and baggage. He will require to be reimbursed."

The Queen hedged. "That will remain to be seen, Sir Francis. It is still possible that the goods, together with the dower of Donna Carlotta, will be recovered and the rogue punished. God's teeth, have I not made myself eminently clear that I will not suffer these unprovoked attacks on Spain to continue. Private gentlemen accused of such practices will stand trial for treason and if convicted will receive no mercy from me. I will listen to no more tales of the threat of Spain. I see none. The Spanish Ambassador must be informed and I will make a full apology to His Majesty for such unwarranted piracy. See to it, Sir Francis."

Walsingham withdrew and the Queen called Sir Robin to her side.

"Now we must consider what is best for Donna Carlotta. Any expense you have incurred is to be listed and forwarded to the controller of my privy purse, sir."

"That will not be necessary, Your Majesty."

She tapped him sharply on the shoulder as he bowed. "Impertinent, sir. You will do as I bid you. I will not have it said that your Queen holds too tightly to her purse strings. Janet Styles was my friend in hard times. I will accept her daughter as her father wished."

Carlotta gave a distressed cry. "Your Majesty, I cannot accept such an honour."

"And why not, pray? You shall be one of my ladies. I have said it, and I wish it."

"I am useless to Your Majesty. I cannot even walk unguided."

"I hear you play the lute and sing passably well."

"I—" Carlotta broke off in confusion.

"You shall entertain me, mistress, more fittingly than some of my empty headed women who make themselves scarce after their lovers the moment my back is turned. I will hear no more excuses. Sir Robin, needs must. You must part with your housekeeper, Martha, for some time longer. She shall sleep with Donna Carlotta as she has done and continue to attend her." She sounded a small handbell, presumably near at hand on a table. "My ladies will guide you into my presence and you will attend me when I need conversation. Indeed you shall improve my Spanish which has become rusty of late." She spoke waspishly to some newcomer who had answered her bell. "Ah, Margaret Whitton, just the girl I wanted. You, at least, have a modicum of sense in your head. This is Donna Carlotta de Rodruigez y Cordoba. She is to become one of my ladies, but she is blind. She will sleep next to you with her maid but you will see to it that she is not left helpless in the corridors and rooms of the palace. You understand—you or one of the other ladies you appoint is to guide her constantly unless she is with her attendant or Sir Robin here."

"Yes, Your Majesty."

"Very well, present yourself later in Donna Carlotta's chamber and for the present see that the steward of the household prepares for her as is proper to a representative of His Spanish Majesty."

"Yes, Your Majesty." The girl withdrew in a rustle of silk.

"Sir Robin, you will stay in attendance."

"Your Majesty."

"We will find some corner in the palace," she chuckled. "I look for some fitting reward—or new poem or song. See to it, sir. Now conduct your lady to the garden until her chamber is prepared and then summon your housekeeper."

Carlotta rose and sank in a curtsey. The royal fingers were extended and lightly touched her hand. She lifted them to her lips.

"Your Majesty is most gracious."

"Ask Sir Robin if you will say that when you have put up with some of my tantrums. Well, let that be, girl. We must wait now until your uncle presents himself at Court, then we can further decide your future."

✿ Twelve

CARLOTTA'S FINGERS gave a final dying chord and then dropped silent into her lap. She waited for the Queen to either commend or make some mark of her disapproval. It was now full summer, early July and the Court had moved to Hampton further from the stinks and plagues

that beset London in the latter months. She had been
summoned to come alone to the Queen's chamber with
her lute, and had been playing and singing for almost an
hour and her throat was beginning to feel the strain.

"The love songs of Spain are either hot and passion-
ate or sad and lingering. They have no knowledge of
moderation, your people. What your mother must have
thought of them I hate to think. She was timid and gentle and yet merry."

"I knew nothing of her, madam. She died soon after
my birth."

The Queen mused, moving fretfully. "She married
her heart's love and bore him a child. Strange he did
not remarry."

"He never forgot her, madam."

"And you do not easily forget him. Still you grieve. I
can hear it in your singing. For him or for Spain?"

"For both, Your Majesty."

"England has no beauty for you?"

"Oh yes, madam, it has held much, kindness and understanding and companionship. Everyone has been
kind."

"Except that bitch, Anne Styles."

"Lady Styles does not approve of me."

"Lady Styles approves of naught that could constitute
a burden."

"That is understandable."

"H'm." The Queen compressed her lips in a sign of
irritation. "What is to be done for you, that is what I
am thinking."

"You tire of my services, madam? I—"

"God's teeth, girl, no, but you cannot remain in attendance on me for ever. I'm thinking of your future."
She paused then said abruptly, "Robin Mallory is mad
for you. You'd best take him."

Carlotta gave a gasp.

The Queen ignored it. "Have you no feeling for him?
Come, miss, don't be shy."

"He has been kind and protective."

"You know he loves you, and that scholar who plays

with the healing art and is made for better things, Martyn Hartington. They'd both have you without dower. Which is it to be? I'd choose Robin." Her voice, softened. "There, I've a fondness for the boy, for all his treasonable talk, God rot him. He apes the fool, but his heart's in the right place and you'd never want."

"Your Majesty, you said yourself I've no dower. How can I be a wife to him, blind as I am, and—well— There are other considerations."

"A man wants a woman who'll not nag him, be undemanding and good in bed. I don't see that any of those abilities require the need for sight. Is there some other man?"

"No—"

"You're over quick to answer me."

"No, indeed, madam."

"Your uncle would have no objection. It would relieve his mind. He's concerned that you'd not be happy at Buckleigh and I agree with him entirely."

"Sir Robin has not spoken of love."

"Of course not. Quite rightly he asked Sir William first if he might address you and then he spoke to me of his intentions. Child, you cannot live with Anne Styles. Do you wish to return to Spain?"

"No, I think not, madam."

"That pleases me. I think you would not be happy in Spain. You look like your father, but you're English at heart."

"But not by faith."

"Your faith is your own business, girl."

"Forgive me, madam, I—"

"Are you a virgin?"

Again Carlotta gasped.

"Well?"

"I—I don't know, madam."

The Queen leaned forward and cupped Carlotta's chin in her hands. "I've heard some excuses in my life from maids who find themselves accused or even with child, but God bless us, not one of them said she didn't know."

"On the ship—"

"Aye?"

"I shared a cabin with the Captain." Carlotta gulped back sudden tears. "He—he did not—take me. He said Spanish blood was not to his taste, but he protected me from the men."

"So, what do you fear?"

"After—after I fell on the quay, I cannot know what happened to me. I do not know whether I was taken by my pursuers back to the ship or how long it was before Sir Robin found me on the beach. Truly, madam, I cannot tell—".

"I see. There is, of course one way of finding out."

"An examination?"

"Yes. Sir Robin should know the truth—or at least be given the right to know, if he so wishes."

"Yes." Carlotta gave a sigh.

"You find the idea of the match distasteful?"

"No—I think I could love Sir Robin. It is just that recently I have become afraid to trust anyone. Believe me, madam, I was not wont to be a nervous, foolish woman."

"I do not think you are one. Few would have striven to conquer your disability as you have done, but you've one abiding fault."

"Madam?"

"Spanish pride. You're stiff-necked, mistress. You fear that what Robin feels for you is not love but pity. Admit it."

Carlotta crimsoned and her fingers caught the lute unaware in her fumbling embarrassment and sent it quivering with discordant sound to the floor at her side.

"Yes, madam, I do admit it."

The Queen reached down in one of her rare gentle movements and stroked her smooth head.

"You are a truly lovely woman, Carlotta, and desirable. I rarely compliment my women so. Their heads are too easily stuffed with their own vain concerns. If you need to be convinced of Sir Robin's motives, the sooner he speaks with you privately the better. Now, child, leave me. I expect Sir William Cecil soon and I must rest before I need to sharpen my wits for the impending battle."

Carlotta rose but as she did so the door opened and she turned uncertainly in that direction. Margaret Whitton's voice carried across the room.

"If you please, Your Majesty, Sir Robin Mallory asked if he might have audience. I told him you expect Sir William Cecil but he says the matter is confidential and will not take long."

"Admit him and Cecil the moment he presents himself."

Carlotta heard the rustle of Margaret's skirts as she curtseyed. "Shall I guide Carlotta back to her chamber, madam?"

"No, wait, child. Sir Robin's business may concern you."

Carlotta waited, her colour heightened as she heard Margaret Whitton's urgent whispering outside, then the sound of Robin Mallory's footsteps and his light voice greeting the Queen.

"Your Majesty honours me greatly."

"Come, Sir Robin. I know you would not badger me without cause. Sit, Carlotta, unless you wish to talk to me alone, sir."

"Madam, Carlotta will wish to hear my news."

"Good, then give it, man. Carlotta and I have been discussing you."

"Madam?"

"Afterwards you will conduct her into the garden. It is fine enough now the storm is over," then testily, "what, what, man, speak out."

Sir Robin had waited patiently to impart it, but his tone betrayed no irritation, only faint amusement which lessened as he passed into the more serious content of his tidings.

"Your Majesty bade me inform you if any information came from Cambridge which might appertain to the abortive attack on Donna Carlotta's life."

Carlotta jerked up her head, gripping her fingers together tightly.

"They have apprehended the assassin?" The Queen was still impatient.

"Alas, no, madam, but the body of one of the players was discovered in an outlying barn. Unfortunately it had not been used for some days and the man has apparently lain dead for some time."

"Peter?" Carlotta framed the question, dreading his answer.

"No, the body is of an older man, about forty. He had only recently joined the company, but played one of the Greek Kings in the performance. He was quite richly clad, though the embroidery was tawdry enough, and it is more than possible that he might answer the description, poor as it was, which Donna Carlotta was able to give us regarding her attacker."

"How did he die?" The Queen rapped out the question.

"From a sword thrust—which passed through his right lung, it would appear."

"Murdered?"

Carlotta could almost imagine his shrug since his tone was casual. "Or as the result of a duel."

"And no sign of the boy?"

"None, whatever."

"Well," the Queen tapped impatiently on her chairarm, a gesture Carlotta had noted as usual when she was impatient or pensive. "We are no nearer the reason for the attack. Could the boy have killed him? Were the members of the company questioned?"

"Yes, Your Majesty, the boy and the older man were new to the company. The boy joined them in some village near the coast, the man much later. He called himself Tom Everard and wished to travel to London. He seemed not inexperienced and they were glad to engage him since another of the company had succumbed to smallpox some weeks previously. After the performance both he and the boy disappeared."

The Queen's foot tapped in time with her fingers. "Do you think the boy killed him, Sir Robin?"

Carlotta leaned forward eagerly. "Your Majesty, I think it most improbable. I knew Peter. He would have been more likely to have been the victim than his dispatcher."

The Queen sighed. "In that case we must look for a third man. Is it likely that this 'player-king' could have been the Captain of the pirate vessel, Sir Robin?"

"His description does not fit that given by Donna Carlotta, Your Majesty. He appears older, thin, not a big man in build, and certainly not red-headed."

"Very curious." The Queen dismissed the matter as it seemed unprofitable to linger on it. "We must leave the whole mystery in abeyance. Like you I consider that *The Kestrel*'s Captain is a wealthier man than this bogus player-actor fellow. If the boy escaped his pursuer he will seek for Donna Carlotta here in Hampton or in London. More and more it seems essential that her future should be in the hands of some capable protector. It is for you to convince her of this necessity and at once. Take her with you, Sir Robin, and do so."

Carlotta rose and curtseyed low. She stooped and retrieved the fallen lute and, as Sir Robin took her hand, backed with him from the chamber.

As the Queen had said, the morning's storm had blown over and with it the sultry heat of the previous days. The garden was pleasantly fragrant, and she eagerly snuffed up the scent of wet earth, leaves and the spicy, scented odours of columbine and musk rose. Sir Robin led her silently, having first disposed of the lute by taking it from her and handing it to a page with instructions to take it back instantly to Donna Carlotta's chamber. He led her to a secluded rose arbour. She knew its position from the faint tinkling music of her favourite fountain. She had grown to know each one by the way its water gurgled into the basin below. Sir Robin assured himself that the wooden bench was not damp and courteously requested that she seat herself.

She made a vain effort to curtail her rising tension,

but outwardly sat calmly, her hands resting quietly on her lap. She had no way of knowing if the pale lilac silk gown she wore today became her and had long since given up worrying about her hair. Teresa had now been restored to her, dashing into her arms with incoherent cries and then later into voluable Spanish when Sir William, his face lined and thin, but apparently in health, returned to London accompanied by Don Miguel Hernandez. Martha and Teresa accepted the presence of each other philosophically, but no woman could be more adequately served than Carlotta and if she did not look her loveliest, it was certainly not due to the negligence of her attendants.

Sir Robin wasted no time. "Lady, both the Queen and your uncle have given me leave to address you. I believe that the Queen may already have spoken to you on this matter."

"Yes." Her answer was whispered but clear enough.

"I have loved you since the earliest days in my house. You could not be unaware of my regard. I believe I can make you happy, Carlotta. I am not of your faith, but I understand it and am tolerant. I will make what provision I can for you to follow its practice. I am a reasonably wealthy man. I hold no position at Court, but in the short time I have known you I do not imagine that you have a craving for power. I can offer you protection and content, peace at Priors Mallory and all my heart, lady. Will you consider the advantages of becoming my wife?"

She was silent and turned her face from him towards the sound of the fountain and her voice appeared to come to him from far away.

"I gain all the advantages from this match, Sir Robin. What do you gain?"

"You." The one word was so vehemently uttered that she trembled in spite of herself. "You are all I want. I shall not press you, rush you into this match without due thought, nor shall I make undue demands on you—afterwards. You can trust me, Carlotta."

She turned back abruptly. "I have been given to

trusting you utterly, sir. Indeed, during these last months I have often wondered how I could exist without your care."

"You do not have to, Carlotta. Have I not made that very clear?"

"Yes, I know you pity me, admire me—but—"

"Do I have to prove I love you?"

She smiled faintly. "I think that you do, sir."

"Stand up." She tilted her head at his order. "Stand up I say."

She obeyed, drawing back a little as he came close and drew her gently into his arms. She nestled close with a little sigh of content then he cupped her chin in his two hands, bent deliberately and kissed her full on the lips. Her own parted soundlessly and she responded, the sweetness of his kiss dispelling her doubts. They remained for some moments close, while he kissed her forehead, her cheek, then stooped to press his lips on the whiteness of her throat.

"Then you will have me, gentle Carlotta?"

She drew away with a forced laugh. "I would be wanton to behave so if such was not my intention." She sought his face with her fingertips and he seized her hand and placed it against his lips. "Dear Robin, I shall pray The Virgin I shall be worthy of you."

"I cannot doubt it."

"Will you take me home soon to Priors Mallory? I love the house so, strange, that of all places I love it best, and I have never seen it."

"As soon as the Queen dismisses us and she will not keep you here against your will."

"She has been so good to me but I feel stifled here and I fear—" She gave a little shudder. "I do not know what there is to fear but—"

"You have had reason to fear in these last months. At Priors Mallory you will be safe. There is not a man, woman, or even animal on the estate who does not love my Spanish girl from the sea."

He felt her quiver in his grasp and she said hurriedly, "Robin, there is one thing you must know. On *The Kes-*

trel the Captain did not—take me." She hesitated before the word then rushed on, "At least I do not think he did, but afterwards, after I fell, I cannot remember and—and I may not be a maid."

"Aye, I am not unaware of the problems."

"The Queen suggested—an examination and I am prepared—if it is your wish—"

"By the Mass, no, sweetheart."

"But it is your right."

"I want you—whatever the circumstances. Tell me 'yes' and I will go to your uncle immediately. We shall be wed without delay. I will not wait one moment for you to have doubts or meet some new gallant who will turn your head with speeches about your hair and your eyes and your fine brows and—"

"Robin, you fool. I am no vain idiot. Alas, I cannot even view my person in the glass. At least I shall save you money on finery. Think of that, my Robin, no demands for a new gown once a month as many wives make." She sobered suddenly. "It is a poor return for the things I cannot do, I cannot oversee the kitchens nor the parlour, nor order the servants. Oh Robin, are you very sure? Suppose, suppose I never see again. Can you bear it?"

"Aye, lass, though I pray God you *will* see again, as Martyn believes, but if it be not the will of God, then I must accept it, as you must bear it, and you will bear it bravely, my little love. I know you and love your courage, but do not think it pity." This last was uttered fiercely and to soften the effect he said more lightly, "Who knows, sweeting, but you may be the loser in the bargain. I have seen you, you may be shocked by the sight of me. I'm no handsome gallant, I tell you now."

"My ears know you, and my fingers know you, and my heart knows you and loves you. Oh Robin, let me not be a disappointment. I am all you get—no dower with me—"

He closed her mouth with his final kiss and led her gently back towards the palace.

🌺 Thirteen

AUTUMN THIS year of 1583 was especially lovely. All at Priors Mallory told Carlotta so and she believed them. For her it meant the delight of sharper mornings, sometimes with a trace of misty dampness on hair and face when she went out into the courtyard but with the mellow rays of the sun kissing her skin in the afternoons, and the crisp crackle and swish of falling leaves underfoot when she dismounted and walked hand in hand with Robin through the woodland to the north of the house, listening to the raucous screech of the sea-birds and the restless cawing of rooks in the elms.

She had returned with a sense of homecoming. From the moment Robin had lifted her down from his saddle-bow, she had felt the comfort of protecting walls once more enclosing her world. She had brought Teresa back with her. Martha had once more to attend to her duties of supervision of the house, leaving Teresa to tend Carlotta as nursling as in the old days in Spain.

One person only had declared dissatisfaction in the match. Miguel Hernandez had come with the Spanish Ambassador to the Court to wish Carlotta well. When his superior had left, Miguel had stood white-faced before his cousin. She could almost feel his antipathy.

"Donna Carlotta, I must give you my best wishes for your happiness."

"Miguel, I am pleased to have you safe. I thank you in the name of our family. You are the only one who will represent my father's family at my marriage."

"I cannot be there, Carlotta," he said coldly, "since it

is your decision to wed this heretic, I have no dispensation to attend the ceremony."

This was one cloud on her happiness. The Queen's chaplain was to marry her but Robin had promised that he would try to find a Catholic priest to bless their union.

"You must understand that priests are forbidden to celebrate Mass since the Pope declared our Queen excommunicated in 1570 and openly stated that no Catholic need remain true to his oath of allegiance. Fines imposed on Catholics who do not attend church services have increased and as many priests, particularly Jesuits, have been found to be implicated in plots against the Queen, many have been arrested, and though there are some still in England, most are in hiding, sheltered by the families who remain true to the old faith."

"Then it is dangerous to seek for a priest?"

"The business must be concluded secretly. My darling, since I know you will not feel our union truly solemnised without such a blessing, I will undertake to find an English priest who will not look askance on your marriage to a heretic."

"He will censure me for that, in all events."

"Possibly, but there are families known to me, Yorkist sympathisers, who will tell me where such a man is to be found."

This, Carlotta was unable to confide to Miguel.

"You love this man?" he said at last.

"I love and respect him, Miguel," she said gently.

"Then I must accept the match, though it is hard."

When he went from her she was conscious of the gulf which had widened between them. On board *The Isabella* she had been aware of his increasing passion. The events of the last months had dissipated none of his feeling for her, and Sir William had told her how night after night the man had tormented himself thinking of her in the hands of the English pirates.

The Queen expressed herself satisfied. Surprisingly, for she was not inclined to generosity, she made Carlotta a marriage gift of fifty gold pieces and a dower chest containing several gowns and a considerable array

of household linen, plates and cups in pewter and a
necklace of amethysts and pearls.

"Had I been in a position to do so, I would have
offered your mother a more suitable marriage gift," she
had said, gruffly, when Carlotta uncertainly stammered
out her gratitude. "The least I can do is to see that her
daughter does not go penniless to her marriage bed." Sir
William Styles had also made her a small present of fine
silver cutlery and plate and an emerald brooch which
had belonged to his mother. He had been somewhat
shamefaced at the need for parsimony, but Carlotta
thanked him sincerely, for she knew his hands were tied
and he not free to treat her as he would wish to do.
Lady Anne held tight the purse strings at Buckleigh.

The ceremony had been simple and Sir Robin had
taken his bride to his own apartment after the private
supper attended by Sir William, Martyn Hartington,
Carlotta's companion ladies, and graced by the Queen
herself. Miguel had also been present with the Spanish
Ambassador.

The Queen had forbidden the usual bawdy revels
which accompanied the bedding of bride and groom.
The noise and unseemly jests would add to Carlotta's
confusion and she was grateful for the Queen's fore-
thought as Martha and Teresa lovingly prepared her for
the arms of her husband.

Robin had been gentleness itself, Carlotta, despite
her determination to yield herself bravely, faced her
marriage night with dread. Her experiences on board
The Kestrel had terrified her, and when Sir Robin
climbed into bed and drew her close, he found her slender body rigid and fearful.

Patiently he stroked her hair and shoulder, gradually
accustoming her to his touch, while he talked laughingly
of some notables who had over-imbibed at supper.
Laughing with him, her constraint lessened and she nestled to him with a little sigh.

Their union was without the fire of passion, but
Robin was content to wait till his bride was ready and
able to surrender herself utterly and he told her, with a

light chuckle, that at all events he had no more doubts as to her virginity.

Flushing in his arms, Carlotta was relieved. Her strict Spanish upbringing had ill-prepared her for the marriage bed, and she knew that Robin had imposed upon himself strict self-control and had considered her inexperience with love and patience.

Now Priors Mallory accepted her as if she had never left and she set herself to learn the position of furniture in every room and to find her way in courtyard and herb garden. Martha encouraged her in management, each day presenting herself for orders and the younger maids obeyed her willingly.

The shortening of the days left long pleasant evenings with Robin before the fire in the parlour, smelling delightfully of apple logs and giving out comforting warmth. Then she would sing to Robin's accompaniment and he began to teach her the art of chess, laughing as their fingers met lovingly on the beautifully carved ivory pieces which had belonged to father and grandfather before him.

Carlotta woke one morning and reached out tentative fingers for her husband's comforting presence by her side. Downstairs she could hear the clink of pewter and buzz of talk but she knew it was yet full early or Martha would have summoned her, since she had given instructions that she was to rise before breakfast, as every mistress would, and oversee the preparation for the meal—yet Robin was not by her side. She sat up, confused, calling his name uncertainly.

He came at once and gave her a smacking kiss which made her sink back laughing on to the pillows.

"You'd missed me. That is what I like to see."

"You are dressing?"

"I am, my love."

"So early? Martha has not called."

"The morning is fair, no mist. I have decided to ride off early."

"Ride, without me?" Her voice betrayed sudden alarm. "But you did not speak of this last night and—"

"I know. As I said I waited for a fair day. I ride North, sweeting—to find you an extra member of the household."

"A priest?"

He checked her instinctive little cry with a light warning finger on her lips.

"I go to visit friends, that is enough. I shall be gone only a few days. I have delayed and should leave now before the winter makes travelling more difficult. You will be safe here with Martha and Teresa."

Again he kissed her, this time lingeringly and her arms stole round his neck and her cheek pressed against his, only to be withdrawn hastily.

"Whiskers—this is new."

"I shall re-grow my beard, sweeting. The sea spray blows chill from the coast. Stay here in bed and let Martha cosset you and do not stray far from the house without escort. Martyn Hartington is back at the rectory. Send to him if there is need."

She let him go from her, resting back and listening to the sound of his steps down the stair, then his voice calling for meat and ale.

When Teresa was preparing her for the day she heard him mount and ride out of the courtyard. She drew a quick breath of fear, then smiled at her own idiocy. In some strange way his departing heralded an end to her idyll and she knew it was her silly woman's doubts that led her to think so.

There was much to keep her busy during the following days, the orchard fruit to be picked and stored, the nut gathering, the autumn slaughter and salting of meat.

Once or twice she had believed that her vision was returning, a sudden greyness where there had been nothing but blackness, a mistiness, but naught had come of it and she had been forced to consider the feeling as nothing but the fantasy result of her dreams and longings. She doubted, and for this reason feared to put the idea to Martyn Hartington when he visited Priors Mallory during the days Robin was gone from her.

She was forced abruptly from her private haven of

dreams and fears by the sudden arrival of Sir William Styles with her cousin, Miguel.

"Niece, you look lovelier than ever and much recovered."

Miguel stooped to kiss her fingers with courtly grace, speaking his greeting in her mother tongue.

"Lady Anne?" Carlotta queried, hesitatingly.

"Alas, niece, Anne will not travel so late in the season. The weather may become inclement without warning, though recently it has been uncommonly warm for October. In all events I have not yet been to Buckleigh. Business kept me in London. I am on my way to Lynn and digressed to greet you."

"You have business there?" Carlotta was puzzled.

"We do indeed. *The Isabella* will be in port there soon. She is to be refitted, why not in London I do not care to think—but there the matter lies. The Queen has expressed a desire to see the damage and speak with Don Pedro, her captain. We go to wait on her, but I have a cousin in marriage living in the town—and Anne has insisted I visit him. She wrote in some haste."

"So you cannot stay here at Priors Mallory?"

"I regret I cannot. Perhaps on the homeward journey if the Queen does not command me otherwise."

"Robin will be sorry you cannot avail yourself of his hospitality. He is away in the North, but I expect him home within a few days, perhaps even tomorrow. Miguel, you will stay, two or even three days—please. It will be so pleasurable for a few days to use my own tongue and there is much I want to hear, of my friends at Court, of the Ambassador, please, Miguel. The ride to Lynn is short. Sir William can ride without you and I need you here."

"If you are sure I shall be welcome."

"You are my dear cousin in blood."

"Then I will accept with delight. I can carry news of your happiness to our relations in Spain. They will want to hear about the house and your place in this new country of yours."

So it was decided. Sir William stayed for dinner then

set off on the last stage of his journey. Martyn Harting-ton had called to discuss some matter with the bailiff and they lingered in the hall together, Carlotta and Mig-uel singing haunting duets, while Hartington applauded. News had come in the afternoon that Robin had com-pleted his business and would be home very shortly. Her happiness was complete. She had come out of the shadows and laughed and chattered in English and Spanish until Hartington wondered that he had ever considered her withdrawn or anxious.

Defying their forebodings that the weather must soon turn foul the following morning dawned as fair as the previous days. Don Miguel rode to the coast early after breakfast and Carlotta set to work with Martha in the still-room. The work of preserving the fruit had also be-gun and the house hummed with pleasant activity. She sat beside Martha while the older woman briskly ex-plained what she was doing in the careful drying of the herbs.

"It is a fine warm day, mistress," she said at last. "Why not go into the garden! There's little you can do here. Everything is under control. I warn you there'll be few more days like this to enjoy. When the winter closes in we shall feel it keenly."

Carlotta rose and reached across the table for the wide flower basket. "There is one dark red rose bush near the wall. I know it because of its sweetness of scent. They tell me there are one or two flowers yet left. I'll gather them for drying."

"You can manage?" Martha paused in her task, un-certain of whether she ought to accompany her mistress. The particular rose bush was right at the end of the gar-den. If Carlotta should stumble—

"I can find it, truly, Martha. I count the steps and follow the wall with my fingertips. I could take your long cane, that helps. I feel with it for the steps and the position of the benches. Let me do something useful. Carry on here. I know you have much to occupy you."

Martha was right. It *was* warm. As she emerged from the house the sun struck hot on her bared head but it

was wonderful to be out. She instructed the dogs to remain in the courtyard. Kendall gave a gentle whine. He
hated to leave her side, but it would be less hazardous
for her if the dogs were not close and liable to get under
her feet.

She walked easily through the courtyard, through the
gate into the herb garden and straight ahead to the gate
which faced it directly into the formal knot garden beyond. Here she must follow the mellow stone wall,
rough under her searching fingertips to the far end
where there was a wooden bench where she could sit for
a while and behind it the sweet-scented roses she
sought.

There was no one in the herb garden or the knot garden. She walked carefully, feeling her way, her light
slippers making little sound on the grass border. She
had stepped from the shingle path because she was liable
to stumble and the grass cushioned her more surely
than the shingle. Once or twice she paused to reach out
for flowers and creepers breaking off leaves and
branches, satisfying herself that she could identify them
and with them, know her position. She knew the far
bench was hidden by the shaped yew trees the garden-
ers pruned with such care, one directly facing the bench
into the form of a gigantic peacock. Robin had described it to her proudly. There she would rest before
returning to the house. Then suddenly she halted. Her
ears had caught the murmur of voices. Someone, no,
two or even more persons, were seated on her bench.
She paused, uncertain whether to proceed since she
hated people to rush to her assistance. She was curious.
It was unlikely to be servants who were much occupied
today about the house and at all events were not allowed to sit about on benches. Since Robin had not returned and Martyn Hartington was not in the house, at
least if he were she had not been informed, she could
not think who was seated there.

She advanced a few paces and immediately had her
answer. The two men spoke in Spanish. Miguel had returned then from his ride but with whom did he talk

here, in her garden? She was about to join him gladly
when the guarded quality of his tone gave her pause.

"I tell you we can speak freely enough here. None in
the house speaks our tongue."

"Donna Carlotta?"

"I have told you, man—she is blind. She will not
venture so far from the house and the old duenna, Teresa, is busy in her apartment. I checked on that some
time ago. In all events, Teresa is not one to walk the
gardens."

"Then I will give you the Ambassador's instructions
and begone immediately. He will arrive in Lynn tomorrow."

"He travels with Her Majesty?"

"No. He was not invited to do so and it did not suit
him to press for the honour."

Miguel grunted. "Just so."

"He will be unexpectedly taken ill tomorrow night
and regretfully inform Her Grace that he cannot accompany her on her inspection of *The Isabella*."

"Wiser so."

"And you—you will go on board?"

"I must."

"The man Styles?"

"Suspects nothing. He will escort Her Grace eagerly.
His indignation concerning the attack is great, especially
since our sufferings after *The Kestrel* left us without ad-
equate crew, thoroughly angered him."

"Don Pedro also endangers himself."

"Like me, he will sacrifice himself willingly if necessary. However I shall watch the situation with care. If it
is possible to withdraw from the close proximity of the
royal party in time, I shall do so and if not—" Miguel
gave an embarrassed barked laugh, "well, I shall have
served the cause. When *The Isabella* explodes she will
take that harlot who reigns on the English Throne with
her. Since the Guise plot failed, we can but try again. I
had not thought so simple a plot possible. She almost
fell into our hands. Is it known how many notables accompany the Queen?"

Horror-struck Carlotta strained her ears for the man's reply but could only partially catch it, ". . . Walsingham goes with her."

"Madre de Dios be praised. He is the one man we could wish would die with her. Cecil?"

"It is not yet known whether he is of the party. He judged the Queen ill advised to ride to Lynn but she had plans to journey to Rising also and she overset his advice. Will you jump—if you can?"

"Aye, if I can." Miguel was silent following the simple sentence. Carlotta's confused thoughts gauged the depths of his decision. She herself was amazingly cool. If anyone could have told her that she would overhear such a conversation and remain silent and without movement she would not have believed it and yet from the first she had been compelled to accept her own danger and keep her terror in check.

The other man was a stranger to her, or she could not identify his voice. He was well-spoken, possibly some gentleman on the Ambassador's staff. The import of his information would have been indeed unwise to entrust to any but loyal gentleman or paid spy.

It appeared that the Spaniard was preparing to leave. She heard him rise and she remained stock-still. Then she heard the two men's steps on the shingle and froze in case they should pass this way. Silently she prayed to the Virgin and it seemed she was answered for they moved away up the far path. She had been sheltered by the yew hedge. They had not known of her presence. She waited for what seemed an interminable interval until she was sure they had left the garden, then forced her trembling limbs towards the bench they had vacated and sat down to consider the implications of what she had heard.

It could not be. She must have misheard. Miguel in a plot to murder the Queen! The Spanish Ambassador implicated! She'd heard and was forced to admit it was clear enough. The men had spoken freely, fearing no eavesdropper who could understand them.

Boldly stated the plan was that *The Isabella* was

primed with barrels of gunpowder. At some given sign when the Queen had boarded, the fuse would be lighted and the ship would explode. Her uncle would be killed with the other members of the royal party. Don Pedro, members of the crew, and even her cousin Miguel would sacrifice themselves willingly if their deaths would help bring about the murder of England's Elizabeth. The Enterprise of England was indeed underway. Philip's ships would come and if some way could be engineered of removing the Queen beforehand, the throne would be vacant, ready for Mary of Scotland.

Carlotta covered her face with her hands. It was unthinkable. She was ashamed of her Spanish blood. Her flesh crawled that she had ever entertained cousinly affection for Miguel or admiration for Don Pedro.

But what could she do? Her first thought was simple enough. She must go back to the house and summon assistance, call Martyn Hartington, rouse the servants, secure the person of Don Miguel—

No—it would not answer. If she were believed, and that was unlikely, the plot would be laid bare and the plotters would abandon Miguel to his fate and go into hiding. The Spanish Ambassador's position would protect him. He would deny everything and exclaim in horror at the suggestion that he could be involved. And if she were not believed—a cold sweat broke out on her body. It might then be too late to save the Queen. Bess, Carlotta knew well, took delight in risking herself to go among the multitude. She would laugh off this threat and go on board *The Isabella,* believing that the Spaniards could not destroy her without harming themselves. She could not remain silent, cower here and let the Queen die. If she told her story to Martyn Hartington could she trust him to take her to the Queen in time, and in leaving Priors Mallory would she alert Miguel's suspicions?

Her duty was clear to her. She must go to the Queen and warn her personally. Elizabeth trusted her as she had her mother, but first she must get to Lynn and with Robin absent the project seemed utterly impossible.

"Carlotta, Querida, where are you?"

Carlotta sat up startled as she heard Teresa's anxious voice from the courtyard. It was imperative that the old woman would not gossip that she had found her nursling in the garden. Miguel must not know that he could possibly have been overheard. Carlotta rose and stumbled forward, her basket and cane forgotten in the need to leave this section of the grounds. She gave a startled cry as she ran slap into a tree. A low branch became entangled in a ribbon on her sleeve and she pulled at it feverishly. It came free with a tearing sound but she hurried on with a half-sob of panic. At last her groping fingers found the archway into the knot garden and she passed inside, pausing to shake out her crumpled skirts and put up a searching hand to smooth her hair. Almost at the same moment Teresa hurried to her side, scolding affectionately.

"Querida, where have you been hiding? You worry me. You should not go so far from the house."

Carlotta laughed, but her voice sounded forced even to herself.

"I have not been far, Teresa. I went to gather roses but I have been lazily sitting in the sun."

"You will roughen your skin, my darling, now come in and rest yourself properly."

Thankful that Teresa had not questioned her about the basket or her postponed walk, Carlotta went meekly inside with her old nurse.

As she presided at table during dinner she strove to appear normal, a hostess delighting in the company of her guest and not by the slightest inflection did Miguel betray the concern about his own future which must have been at the forefront of his mind.

He intends to kill himself, Carlotta told herself. He knows that it is unlikely that he can escape. Even if he is able to jump, as planned, he will be very close to *The Isabella* when she explodes. He chats and laughs as if he is unaware that tonight might be his last on earth.

Her fingers fumbled on the rim of her Venetian crystal goblet and the wine spilled. She felt its wetness be-

tween her fingers. Miguel exclaimed and called for a
servant. She apologised somewhat shakily for interrupt-
ing his talk.

"You seem pale, Carlotta. Do I tire you?"

"No, indeed. I have enjoyed having you with me. I
shall miss you. Must you leave early?"

He gave a sigh of what she believed to be genuine
regret. "I must rise with the sun. I shall take meat and
ale at an inn and change into my splendid clothing to
meet the Queen."

"Do you return with the Ambassador's party?"

Was it her imagination or did she detect a stiff note
in his answer.

"Yes, I shall rejoin the Ambassador's staff. I sail for
Spain with dispatches within a few days, so do not be
alarmed if you do not hear from me."

"You sail from Tilbury then?"

"From Lynn if there is a vessel in port available for
the Netherlands. From there I can take ship for Cadiz.
The Ambassador informs me by message that the dispatches are urgent and should reach His Majesty as
soon as possible."

"Then you received a messenger? Here?"

"One came earlier this afternoon. I think you may
have been sleeping."

"I regret I did not know of his arrival. I would have
made him welcome. I trust you offered him refresh-
ments, cousin."

"He was in haste. I thank you but he bade me give
you the good wishes of the Ambassador."

She inclined her head in answer. "Since you make an
early start it would be well if we retire early."

He rose and came up behind her chair. "Let me help
you."

As he reached out and took her hand she steeled herself not to recoil from his touch. He led her from the
room to the foot of the stair and stopped to kiss her
fingers. His own lingered on hers and she allowed them
to do so, then as Teresa came soft-footed to her side,
she bade him good night and mounted the stairs.

She sat on the bed clutching her hands so tightly together that the nails of the one bit cruelly into the other. She had sat there with the traitor and coolly made conversation and the minutes of the Queen's life were ticking away inexorably.

What could she do? Could she send for Hartington and beg him to escort her to Lynn? Such conduct would alert Miguel's suspicions. Why then—what mattered if the Queen's life was saved? But would it be? Miguel was desperate enough to risk his own life in this venture. He would allow nothing to stand in his way now. If he guessed—even dreamed that she knew of this proposed assassination he would kill her. The thought came like a douche of ice-cold water. He would kill her—though he loved her.

She put a hand to her mouth to prevent an involuntary sob. Yes, Miguel loved her. She knew that. On *The Isabella* he had made his feelings plain—then later in the first angry outpourings of bitterness when she had told him of her coming marriage to Robin. This was his one weakness. He would give his soul to possess her—and he had little time.

If she could make Miguel believe that she returned his love he would take her with him to Lynn and that was her one hope. But not yet. She had all night to consider. In the morning she would join him somewhere en route. She would make him believe she longed to return to Spain. It would not be easy. Miguel was no fool, but he was in no rational state. His own position was desperate. He would believe what he wished to believe. It would be his last comfort. Naught would turn him from his sworn purpose but he would hold Carlotta in his arms just once before he died.

Yet even this she could not accomplish alone. Blind as she was she could not journey out of the house without assistance. Someone must aid her—Teresa. But the old woman would panic if she knew the truth. She would scream and beg Miguel not to go on board *The Isabella*. She would betray to him what they knew, before the party reached Lynn. Therefore Teresa must not

be told. She must believe, like Miguel, that Carlotta desired to flee her husband's house for her lover's arms.

Carlotta heard the old woman stir in the room next
to her own. She went to the door and called quietly.

"Teresa."

Her nurse came at once, concern making her voice
unaccountably sharp.

"What is it, Querida? Can you not sleep?"

"Close the door. Come close."

Impatiently Carlotta drew the old woman on to the
bed.

"Did you hear Don Miguel? He leaves England
soon."

"Aye, I heard him."

Carlotta gave a little sob, and there was no pretence.
The thought of her handsome cousin lending himself to
such a deed and the possibility of such a death filled her
with horror.

"I cannot let him go."

"Querida?" Teresa was incredulous, dismayed.

Carlotta clawed at her arms. "I cannot stay here in
England. I want to go with him, Teresa. I must return
to Spain. Here I shall stifle."

"Querida, I thought you happy here, content: That
you loved your husband."

"He has been good to me. I was content until—until
Miguel came. Now——" She broke down and sobbed, the
tears running through her fingers on to the old woman's
gnarled hands. "I have always loved Miguel. On the
ship—we met secretly. I thought he would be killed.
Our love seemed fated in all events since he was betrothed. I thought never to see him again and the Queen
wished me to wed Sir Robin."

Teresa drew the weeping girl close into her arms, the
voice muffled by the sobs.

"There will be war, Teresa. Everyone predicts it.
Miguel will go. I cannot remain in this cold land where
soon all will despise me." Her fingers clutched at the
stuff of Teresa's gown. "I will leave with Miguel tomorrow, before Sir Robin returns. You will help me?"

"My loved one, do you know what you do? Are you sure?"

Teresa's only answer was a nod, while Carlotta stilled her tears and waited anxiously for her answer.

"You will sin against Holy Church. You leave your husband for a lover. Don Miguel cannot wed you—"

"He will provide for me. He will take me home. Please—Teresa."

There was a long silence. Carlotta listened to her nurse's heavy breathing. She could imagine the tortured expression on the beloved nut-brown face.

"Then if you must, you must," Teresa muttered, "though The Virgin knows I would wish things different. He is prepared?"

"No." Carlotta gasped out the word, feverishly clinging to Teresa's hands. The one thing she did not want was for Don Miguel to be warned in advance of her intention to accompany him. He would consider the matter, and his conscience would cause him to repudiate her. Despite his natural desires he would refuse to implicate her. No, he must be taken by surprise. Without time to think and in the cold sweat of fear which would envelop him tomorrow he would agree to their flight.

"He is too honourable. He will put my future before our love. He must not be told."

"But—"

"Very early you will dress me and get me out of the house. We will wait for him on the Lynn road. Once he knows I have burned my boats behind me, he will be forced to agree—and he *must*."

She gave Teresa a little shake of determination and the old woman grunted.

"It is as you say. The Virgin guide you into a change of heart."

"You would have me live among heretics?"

"I would have you live an honourable wife. Love, you are not completely whole—suppose he should take you for a while only, and then abandon you. Have you thought of that?"

"Of nothing else, dear Teresa. But I love him and I trust him."

As Teresa moved to leave her she put out a detaining hand.

"Sleep with me tonight. I'm afraid."

They lay together consoling each other by nearness. In the darkness Carlotta prayed for the strength and cunning to convince Miguel as she had done Teresa. Her thoughts dare not range beyond her set purpose of the morning. Of Robin she could not allow herself to think at all.

🏵 *Fourteen*

THE MORNING was chilly though dry and Carlotta shivered under her warm cloak, pulling the concealing hood more closely under her chin as she sat her docile mare, patiently waiting with Teresa under the shelter of the small copse at the extreme northern edge of her husband's estate. They had managed to reach the ground floor without accident, though neither Carlotta nor her maid were as sure-footed as they had been. Carlotta waited in an agony of dread while Teresa tried the main door of the hall. It was barred but well oiled in the hinges. After some grunting the Spanish woman had the door open and had come back to guide her charge towards the stable.

Here they had encountered their first difficulty. Teresa was no horsewoman and Carlotta, handicapped as she was, unable to saddle their horses. After some consideration she had decided to rouse the groom. The plan would be useless without his assistance.

Even now she broke out into a cold sweat as she remembered her cool explanation.

"Jed, saddle Jenny for me and the mare for Teresa. We've decided to accompany Don Miguel part of the way into Lynn."

The boy had been incredulous, half bemused by sleep. "Mistress, Don Miguel does not plan to leave for another hour at least—"

"I wish to surprise him and will meet him on the road."

"You'll want me to ride in attendance, mistress—"

"No." Her refusal was fast, too fast. She felt his shocked amazement and corrected herself. "It isn't necessary. We ride only to the main Lynn road and will be back by mid-morning. Teresa is with me and the horses gentle enough."

The boy made no more objections and within minutes they had mounted and were on their way. Teresa took her bridle rein and drew her into the copse. Indeed she knew her way no further. Here they waited for the sounds which would herald Don Miguel's departure.

She bit her lip nervously. What could she say to him—how convince him of her love? He must take her to Lynn—he must. After that it would be up to her to contrive a way of reaching the Queen.

She stiffened as she heard the noise of the approaching horsemen.

"Go to the gap in the trees. Make sure it is them."

"Querida—"

"Go—or leave me."

Teresa gave a little strangled sob then Carlotta heard her urge her mare forward. She waited as the horsemen drew closer, then there came a startled exclamation. They were too far away for Carlotta to hear what was said, then there was a flurry of hooves. A man drew up his horse, dismounted and came to her. Strong arms enfolded her waist.

"Carlotta, querida. Is it what she says? You wish to go with me?"

Carlotta's small moan was real enough. "Miguel, oh Miguel, I need you. It *is* you?"

"It is, my sweet child. Why did you not speak of this yesterday? You know my heart has longed for you."

Anxious to avoid his embrace she urged him to a remembrance of their danger.

"Later, Miguel. Now we must leave the vicinity of Priors Mallory. Let me mount with you. It will be quicker."

His lips brushed her cheek. "My heart, we must discuss this, but as you say not now, not here. I cannot believe that—no matter. Diego must take Teresa behind him. We'll leave your mounts here. Up with you, my sweet girl—and we'll ride hard for the coast."

As once she had ridden with Robin, she clung tightly to Miguel's slim waist. The speed of the ride forced all other thoughts into abeyance. It needed all her concentration to remain mounted. Once aware of the need Miguel rode hard and fast. She had no time even to question that he had accepted her presence so readily. Miserably she was aware that he too snatched at a brief joy without consideration of the future. At last Carlotta heard cobbles under the horses' hooves and knew they had arrived. She was stiff and cold when Miguel lifted her down in the courtyard of the inn where he had told her he would breakfast and change into finery fit to greet the Queen.

He said quickly, "Wait outside for one moment only while I examine this place and see that it is safe for you. Teresa is here."

She huddled against her old nurse while she felt him withdraw and confer softly with his servant, then she heard them both enter the inn. Teresa was about to speak, make one more appeal. If so, Carlotta was in no mood to heed it. She gave a cautioning hiss, as almost at once, Don Miguel returned to her side.

"Come, all is arranged. There are two chambers above the tap-room. The smaller one will serve for me as a changing room. In the other you must wait for my return." His voice altered only slightly yet she caught at his heightened tension. "We have time yet before I need to prepare. Let me help you inside and to mount the stairs."

Climbing was an ordeal since the staircase was in need of repair and rickety. Carlotta gave the difficulty scarcely a thought while her mind juggled with the problem ahead. Too well she knew she must soon submit herself to Miguel's love-making. It could not be delayed if she were to convince him of her sincerity. Even this disturbed her less than her anxiety for the Queen. It was essential that Miguel should take her with him when he boarded *The Isabella* and this he would *not* be prepared to do.

He drew her solicitously to a wooden settle. She felt the chill wind from the sea. Obviously the window was open. They were yet early and there were few people stirring in the streets. Miguel was talking and she forced her attention back to him.

"How soon do you expect Sir Robin?"

"What?" She had dismissed her husband from her mind in the greater concern for her mission.

"Sir Robin? He will attempt to pursue."

"I—I do not know. It may be some days. He is in the North. How soon do we sail for the Netherlands?"

"Today if I can manage it." Was it her imagination that picked up his hesitancy. "I had not expected to leave so soon. Yet it can be done."

"Is the Queen lodged in the town?"

"I think not. Her progress was reported slow. She stayed in Cambridge. I know not at whose house she slept last night."

"Do you think she will order repayment for the damage?"

"She has expressed a willingness to do so. I confess her agreement has surprised me."

"She has been good to me."

"True, she treated you kindly. She felt in honour bound to discharge her debt."

"Sir William will be in the town."

"Aye."

"If he should see me——"

"He must not, yet awhile."

"Do you go early to greet him?"

"I must do so." He came closer and she sensed his agitation. "You remind me we have so little time." He called impatiently. "Teresa, leave us. Your mistress will require breakfast. See that it is prepared with care but do not disturb us for an hour."

Anxious to prevent Teresa's objections, Carlotta made her own voice sharp. "Please obey Don Miguel implicitly. I wish it."

Teresa knew that imperious tone only too well. Carlotta heard the rustle of her curtsey and the sound of the door latch as she withdrew. She steeled herself for his embrace, but he was tender, drawing her to her feet, and kissing her fingers, then her wrists, then her eyes and finally her lips. She forced herself to lie quiescent in his arms, but he sensed her withdrawal and drew from her, holding her at arms' length, his hands on her shoulders.

"What is it? Are you afraid? We cannot be interrupted."

"Give me time, cousin."

His answer was rough. "We have little time. In just over an hour I must leave."

"But you will return. I am wearied. We have all our lives."

"The Virgin grant it so." She caught the faint mutter.

She reached up to feel for his face with her fingertips. "What is it, Miguel? You frighten me. What do you mean?"

He strove to appear normal. "Forgive me, love. I am impatient. I cannot believe you will be mine and I fear ill fortune might still rend you from me."

She gave a little laugh. "You are foolish. What could part us now?"

"Styles could demand your return to your husband. The Queen would be angered if she guessed at your presence here."

Carlotta bit her lip in exasperation. For this reason

alone she would not be allowed near to the Queen. Her last hope lay in sending some message to Sir William Styles after Don Miguel had left. How, she could not yet think. She could not write and Teresa had little English, yet Teresa had opportunity to leave the inn. Indeed Miguel would wish her safely out of sight but Teresa had been dismissed for an hour. How to recall her without arousing suspicion?

She swayed suddenly in his arms and he caught her close. "You are ill?"

"No, just the excitement of the ride and I slept ill. I am tightly laced. Lead me to the bed, Miguel."

He obeyed immediately. She sank down and pulled him down to his knees close by her.

"My love, be patient for just a little time. Will you leave me and send Teresa up to me here?"

"But—"

She felt the warm flush dye her cheeks as she whispered, "She will help me undress. I am clumsy in my blindness, I need her."

"I will act as tire-woman."

"No, Miguel. I will not have it so. Give me only minutes and I will be ready for you and beautiful. Please—"

Her tone was coaxing and he gave way.

She caught her breath abruptly as he left her and called to the old woman below.

Teresa was hard pressed from the climb. Hastily Carlotta bade her unlace her.

"Querida—"

"Do as I bid you. Come close and listen. We have little time. You must leave the inn when I dismiss you and seek out Sir William Styles."

"Leave you here alone?"

"Yes. I do not know where he lodges but enquire of the innkeeper of any wealthy man who has recently received a visitor from court, within the last few days. You understand? I do not know his cousin's name. It is imperative you find him."

"But—"

Carlotta drew her close. "You must not fail me. If necessary await him on the quay."

"I do not understand. I thought you wished to avoid seeing him. Don Miguel—"

"Sir William is not to go on board *The Isabella* nor is he to allow the Queen to do so. If they do not heed this warning they will both die."

"My darling—this cannot be—"

"Teresa, it *is* so. He *must* believe you. He speaks some Spanish. You must convince him—any way possible. There is danger for all who board *The Isabella*. Over and over again tell him that. I cannot write and Miguel will not let me near him."

Teresa appeared suddenly calm. "Then this is why—"

"Yes, I *dared* not tell you before. You will not fail me?"

"If I leave you with him—"

"It is a small price to pay. Knock on his door. Wait until the servant is off guard and go. Be careful. Do not question the innkeeper while the Spaniard is listening. I trust no one."

Teresa bent forward and kissed her gently, then she moved away. Carlotta heard her quiet scratching on the neighbouring door and Miguel's equally soft reply. She lay back against the pillows. Teresa held the Queen's life in her hands, She, Carlotta, must now keep Miguel occupied until the old woman got clear from the inn. The room seemed oppressive. Noise had increased in the street. People were awakening. She heard shutters unbarred. Miguel delayed, or did it only seem to be a long time before he came to her? She forced herself not to jump as he sat down by her side.

"Carlotta, listen, my heart. Do you believe that I love you?"

"I trust you with my future."

His voice was thickened. "You may not be wise. No—" he checked her startled rejoinder. "Listen and do not halt me, not yet. I want you. I always have, but there are reasons why—" he groped for words, "why I am concerned that my treatment of you is not honourable. For reasons I cannot disclose I may be unable to protect you—afterwards."

"In Spain—"

"I will take you home. All will be well. Your welfare, should we reach Spain, will be assured. Carlotta, I may not return to you, here at the inn."

"But—"

"If I do not, know that I would have given my soul to do so and forgive me. There is gold in my saddle-bags. Yours must be the choice. Either cast yourself on the protection of the Spanish Ambassador—or return to your husband, for if I do not return by noon, I shall never do so."

"Miguel—"

"Do not ask me, my heart. If you love me, give me yourself. Do I ask too much?"

"I have promised."

She was trembling violently but he judged her distress due to his words of ill-omen. Her mouth opened under his kiss and his arms caught her to him. She thanked The Virgin she had not to see his face, now was he in any state to guess at her utter revulsion. Her arms stole round his neck and he thrilled to her touch. In her love he would take his temporary comfort.

She paid no attention to the increased noise below. The inn seemed to be receiving custom, fishermen possibly, or tradesmen anxious to drink before beginning the day's stint of labour.

Miguel gave a muttered curse as feet clattered up the stair. These rooms were privately hired. Why had the fool of an innkeeper allowed intruders to mount to them?

Carlotta gave a cry of alarm as the heavy door received a crashing blow as if some object had been thrown heavily against it. Miguel released her and stood up.

"The Spanish gentleman, and engaged, I see."

Carlotta went white to the lips. She drew back to the wall against which the bed had been set. She made no outcry, and taken by surprise, nor did Miguel for the first minutes of the encounter. She knew that voice, had dreamed of it in nightmares, the English Captain's, and Miguel knew him well enough.

He blustered in fury, his fluency deserting him.

"Nombre de Dios, what do you here? Your presence is an affront to decency. Get out."

"And if I choose not to?"

"I'll call the watch and turn you over to the Queen's officers for the pirate cur you are, or—"

"Or—my friend?" The cheery voice prompted. "You'll do what? Kill me? I am afraid you will have to. I regret if it distresses the lady, but you must see I am here to protect my interest. I have heard talk of reprisals. *The Isabella* is to be inspected and refitted. I cannot allow that. She is my prize. She will slip her moorings and be lost before the Queen enters Lynn."

"No." Carlotta heard herself scream. "Your men must not board her."

"Ah, lady, you are concerned for the Spanish crew? Again I express regret, but what must be, must be."

"The ship is primed with barrels of gunpowder. She will explode."

Miguel gave a snarl of fury. In a flash of comprehension he knew her reasons for coming to him. He hit her hard and called her a filthy name in his own tongue.

"So you betray your faith, by your body, slut."

She nursed her bruised cheek in her shame.

The Englishman gave a word of command. The movement of feet told her Miguel was surrounded and she knew he was not armed. He had come to her half-clad.

She heard only one more command, "Take him."

There was a scuffle, a sharp cry of pain, then Miguel said no more. A slithering sound told her he was being dragged along the floor. The men who accompanied their captain did not speak at all.

She lay still waiting for him to leave her alone. She had no doubts he would believe her warning. She knew her man. He would take no chances, for his own crew, or for the Queen. Elizabeth would be safe.

Miguel was hustled down the stair. There seemed no opposition. Did even the innkeeper and the servants do this man's will? Were they in his pay? How had he known where to find his man? Her thoughts raced with the inconsistencies. Teresa—had he seen the old woman in the street? Had she babbled of the plot? Had he indeed known of it already? Now, now by the body of Christ, why did he delay, why did he not leave her alone in the room?

Suddenly his voice cut across her horrified stillness.

"I suggest you dress, lady." She remained stupefied and he said, "I think you understand me well enough. Dress and be ready to accompany me."

"I don't understand. Why should I go with you anywhere?"

His reply was a half-sneer. "If you prefer to answer to Sir Francis Walsingham's men, concerning your part in this attempt on the Queen's life, you may remain here. I do not advise it. Their methods are not gentle, as the Spanish Don will find to his cost."

She gave a haughty rejoinder at his implied accusation.

"How dare you, sir. I know nothing of this affair. Sir Francis would not dare touch me. Indeed he is known to me as is Her Grace the Queen, to whom you will answer, both for your treatment of me on *The Isabella* and if you dare use me ill, now."

He gave a short barked laugh. "Sir Francis would hand his grandmother to the executioner if he suspected her of treason. Do not trust to his friendship. You *knew* of the plot. You warned me."

Carlotta swallowed, sick with apprehension.

"I know only what I told you, nothing more. I sent my duenna, Teresa, to warn Sir William Styles. You may find her nearby. Question her if you must. Leave me and go about your business. Do you dare delay, sir? The Queen must not board *The Isabella*."

"Have no fear, lady. She will not. That has already been arranged. As for your maid, she was not near when we entered. We cannot wait for her. My men will escort you by road to Snettisham. *The Kestrel* is lying anchored off the coast. They'll take you aboard from Snettisham beach." He moved impatiently nearer. "For God's sake, madam, do as I bade you. Hasten and dress."

"I'll not come with you. I am the wife of Sir Robin Mallory. He will kill you if you lay hands on me."

He gave a great booming laugh which echoed in the low raftered inn room.

"Mallory's wife—you? By the Saints, that's rare news."

"What mean you, sir?" she snapped.

"You are a rare parcel of Spanish passion for our poetic country gentleman. However, we'll not talk of that now. Had you thought to explain to him why you were found in the Spaniard's arms?"

"What I tell my husband is my own business, none of yours. How many times must I order you to get out and leave me to wait for my maid's return?"

"No more times. I'm losing patience. I've ordered you to dress, or do I take you as you are?"

His threat carried weight and she trembled, rising panic and anger fighting common sense.

"Fool, I cannot dress without help. Can you not see, I'm blind."

"Blind?" He stooped and fiercely took her by the shoulders. She felt his breath fan her cheek while he examined her face at close quarters, then let her go.

"God's mercy, lady. I did not know."

She raged at the quieter tone of his answer. "If you did not, it's passing strange, since my blindness can be attributed to your actions. A blow on the back of my head when I fell against the quay wall in my escape from your ship, was the cause of it, my doctor tells me. Have you the effrontery to kidnap me once more against my will?"

"Aye, madam." His tone was curt. "And I'll wait no longer." He bent and picked up the coverlet. "Wrap yourself in this, while I call to my men below."

"I'll not go." She forced back the threatened tears. He paid no heed and she reached out helplessly for the silk of her gown and in frantic haste donned it, leaving laces and stomacher untightened, then obediently pulled round her the coverlet he had thrust near to her grasp. She had no knowledge of where Teresa had placed her cloak and there was no time. This man would not hesitate to carry her half-naked through the inn if she delayed longer.

He grunted his approval when he came back from the door.

"I'll carry you below."

It was useless to argue further and she allowed him to lift her easily and descend the stair. Her ears gave no indication of the presence of the innkeeper or his servants in the passage and she was thankful for this mercy as he placed her down on her feet and issued his orders to his subordinates.

"Convey the lady to the ship. Guard her well until I come. I go to the quay."

"The Spaniard?" The seaman's question was devoid of emotion.

"Leave him with Walters and myself. Later I'll give him into official hands."

"Aye, sir."

"Treat the lady with courtesy and care. She is blind. You'll answer to me for her well-being."

The seaman placed a firm but respectful hand on her elbow. Carlotta swung blindly towards the spot where she believed the Captain to stand, for one final appeal, but already he had moved away and she heard him from a room along the corridor talking briskly to some serving man or tap-room wench. She did not catch the reply. She bit her lip and blinked back angry tears. For a second it seemed that her weak and foolish limbs would not obey her and the seaman would be forced to carry her, then their trembling stopped and she went with him. Outside he had a carriage waiting. He helped her inside, called an order and climbed in beside her.

🍂 *Fifteen*

CARLOTTA STUMBLED and fell heavily for the tenth time. She caught back a sharp cry of pain and pulled herself up warily. The cabin was alien. She had been a fool to get up from the chair again.

The seaman had carried her aboard and below since she could not have traversed the decks with their litter of tackle, blockage and rope. That had been some two hours after noon and it seemed hours since he left her to herself. Some time ago he had knocked on her door and asked if she required food or wine. She had sent him away though she thanked him. The man had been kind enough and offered her no discourtesy.

Her searching fingers found the bed post and explored the silken coverlet. Thankfully she drew her bruised body on to its comforting length. She had discarded her makeshift cloak and her hair still streamed down her back uncoiled. She had no combs or pins. She must leave it as it was. Her dress must be creased and perhaps soiled. She drew it off and threw it from her. Her head ached with the unsolved problems she put to herself. She slipped back against the pillows and allowed herself the relief of tears.

She tried not to think of Miguel. What the English Captain had said regarding Sir Francis Walsingham was true enough. He would be ruthless with enemies of the State. Miguel would be put to the question. The Spanish Ambassador would not be able to help him and afterwards—he would die, terribly. She told herself he had meant to destroy the Queen and with her many innocent lives. He deserved his fate, yet according to his be-

liefs and allegiance he had done his duty. She crossed
herself and prayed for him, tears spilling down on to
her clasped hands.

Absorbed in her prayers she was startled to hear the
key scrape and the door was thrust open. She remained,
half kneeling on the bed, and the captain spoke from
the doorway.

"God, but you're beautiful."

As he slammed the door to and advanced, she cried,
"What do you want?"

He waited before replying then bent forward and
lifted a long strand of dark red hair and smoothed it
through his fingers.

"What the Spaniard wanted, presumably what Sir
Robin Mallory wanted."

"No." The single word sounded feeble, childish, yet
she could find nothing else to say.

He caught her to him fiercely and thrust back her
head, then bent and kissed her throat.

"Why not—you're not now so virginal or was I mistaken in what I saw in the inn chamber? It *was* Sir
Robin you said you married?"

The sneering tone, thickened with desire, jarred on
her senses. She reached out to strike at his face and he
held her with one shoulder while he forced down her
wrists with his freed hand

"You would not dare."

"Why not?"

"The Queen—Sir Robin—"

"Neither are here, my lovely. I spared you once." His
tone now seemed mocking, less condemning. "I swore I
didn't want you, Spanish flesh and inexperienced to
boot. It's not so now. You're a wife and presumably a
lover."

"I love my husband. Please—"

He laughed at her tearful pleading.

"You'll have me believe that when I found you in the
Spaniard's arms? Come, Querida, be honest with yourself and me."

"He wanted me. He would have taken me because—

because he knew he was to die. I led him on. I *wanted* him to believe I loved him, that way he brought me to Lynn—near the Queen. I—".

His lips silenced her effectively. She was unable to draw breath as her own were thrust apart bruised on to her teeth. She struggled helplessly, but his weight was heavy on her body and she was exhausted.

He stripped her easily and took her brutally. She was spent with fear and shock. Her experience with Robin had ill prepared her for this fierce, elemental desire which slaked itself regardless of her suffering or resistance.

He left her at last while she turned on her side and sobbed into the pillows. She heard him slop wine into a goblet and drink deep. For a while he left her alone and she dared not move or attract his attention. At last she heard him come to the bed. She moved blindly away from him as he threw himself down beside her. One arm was flung possessively across her body, drawing her tight into his embrace, and when he slept, she lay wakeful, dry-eyed.

When, hours later, he stirred, she shuddered and he traced a finger gently round her cheeks and lips.

"You are cold. Let me cover you."

"No." She pushed back his hand. "Let me lie. Don't touch me."

He was still for a moment then he said, "Come, lass, I'm sorry. Events had stirred me. You're none the worse for this. I've not harmed you."

"You have soiled me." She grated out the words one after the other, slowly, through her teeth.

He got up and went to the table again.

"Drink some wine, you'll feel better."

He thrust the goblet against her teeth and she angrily pushed away his hand, spilling the wine.

"I'd not thought you so new to the game. Your husband has spoilt you."

"He is considerate."

He replaced the wine goblet and sat down by the bed.

"It might be one way of putting it."

"He is not a beast."

"Which I am?"

"I leave you to judge yourself. Are there not women who will take you but those you must force?"

"And does only Spanish blood attract you?"

"I told you. Miguel meant naught to me. I overheard him talking of the plot. None would believe me. I had to get to Lynn. It was the only way. Why should I defend my conduct to you, thief, dirty scum of a pirate?"

"That's better," he laughed softly, "you're recovering your spirits. Blind or no you're still a little cat with claws and lovely, more lovely than you were. Marriage has heightened your charms."

"Miguel," she said abruptly, "what of Miguel?"

"He's dead. I'm sorry to put it so baldly but it's all I can do."

"They killed him? He died under torture?"

"No. He chose to die his own way. He swam to the ship. He fought free of my men, plunged into the water in an effort to warn the Spanish Captain."

"My men had fired the ship after casting her loose. We gave the Queen a rare sight when she entered Lynn." He sighed heavily. "Those Spaniards have a liking for fire. It was perhaps an easier death than in Walsingham's private cells in the Tower, simpler to explain to his Catholic Majesty, an unfortunate accident. The Queen is relieved."

Carlotta did not question his wisdom. She accepted the simple truth of it. Both Don Pedro and Miguel would have preferred the end to come as it had, and as the Captain had said, it saved explanations.

"And the Ambassador?"

"Ah," the Captain's tone was grimly amused. "He did not ride with Her Grace. Some trifling ailment kept him in London."

"Sir William Styles?"

"Had been promptly warned. Your duenna, by the way, is on board. One of my men found her at the inn afterwards, distractedly enquiring for you."

"You took her prisoner?"

"She came of her own volition, anxious to find you."

Carlotta knew this to be true. Teresa's one thought would be for her.

The Captain had moved from her again. She moved her head, attempting to place him. Returning he guided her hands round the rim of a second goblet.

"Now drink. You need it."

Obediently she lifted the cup to her lips. He was right, she was spent and suddenly cold. When he took the cup from her she sat biting her nether lip to prevent its trembling. As if aware of her need he moved round her side of the bed and stooped to adjust the crumpled bed-clothing then attempted to pull them up round her.

"Lie back and rest."

She resisted him and he took her shoulders, exerting gentle pressure in order to place her down as he had commanded. He felt her terrible shivering and held her close in an effort to comfort.

"Don't, lass, don't cry. I'll not hurt you again. I swear it."

"Two brave men dead— and for what?" She sobbed weakly against his shoulder and he stroked her hair.

"He did not suffer—Miguel or the Captain? Tell me—"

"It was very quick. They could have felt nothing."

"Thank God. Oh thank God."

"You loved him?" His question was very soft but clear enough.

"No, but he loved me. I knew it long ago. I caused his death."

"I think not."

"But—"

"I came seeking him. We—" he corrected himself carefully, "some friends of mine suspected treachery. That the Dons should invite the Queen aboard one of their ships was unusual. She was advised to refuse, but the Queen allows no man to persuade her. He was prepared to die in the explosion. He confessed as much. Mourn him if you will but not holding yourself in any sense to blame."

Her weeping ceased and she drew from him, as if aware that his nearness now disturbed her. He let his hand fall from her hair and she waited tremulously for him to rise. For moments they stayed so, then with a little incoherent cry he drew her to him, this time with infinite tenderness.

She made an ineffectual attempt to release herself, but in later moments she knew it was half-hearted. She needed his comfort and he was close and strong and dependable. With a little sob she surrendered into his arms and her lips parted under his sweetly.

He made no effort to force her and she quietened under his caresses. At last he let her go and she put her hands to her face as if to hide herself from him.

"You must go. Please—please go. I have sinned, sinned greatly."

"You needed me. I was there. That is all there is to it. Rest, in the morning all will be well."

"What—what will you do with me?"

He checked in his walk across the cabin. "Do with you? Why, smuggle you back to your husband's house."

"You'll let me go, now?" Her cry was sharp.

"What else can we do? He may not have returned. If he has, then your duenna will be with you. Will she not lie if there is need?"

"I *cannot* go back to him."

"You must."

She winced at the simplicity of his answer. "Take me with you."

He came back to her and took her hand in his own. "Querida, I cannot do that, and in your heart you do not wish it."

"I cannot lie to Robin."

"There is no need. Say nothing of this. Why should he doubt you?"

"You talk as if there is naught between us."

Again his reply jarred on her strained hearing. "But there *is* naught. I took you by force. You have not betrayed him. He will believe what you tell him. You are his wife. You must return. You have no choice."

She caught at his hand, now desperate to prevent him leaving. "You have the choice. I can sail with you. You lie when you say you forced me, at first, yes—later— If there should be a child?"

She felt his shrug. "If so, naught can be proved."

"My God, you are cruel."

"Querida, be sensible. You do not love me. At this moment I have stirred your senses. You are distraught. Any man who comforted you at such a time would seem to capture your heart. You are no green maid, but a true woman, wed and bedded. Mallory is your husband."

"You fear to take me from him."

"I will be frank. What use can you be to me—a blind girl, rather a hindrance."

She gasped as if he had struck her. Indeed if someone had douched her in icy water it could not have been more effective than his words. She turned her head abruptly from him.

"Leave me. Send in Teresa."

"Love, be sensible. I live by my wits. I am a thief and a pirate and my life is forfeit the first false move I make. If I am captured, what then? Mallory offers you protection. He's a fine man. He deserves you. As soon as it's light. I'll row you ashore. The carriage will take you to Lynn. It will convey you back to the inn and the landlord will say what I bid him. You came to Lynn in search of Sir William Styles and to try to see the Queen. She will have left the town, but no matter. Your story will be believed. Styles will escort you to Priors Mallory. Your duenna will be with you. She will swear she never left your side. What is there to fear?"

"And you?"

"I sail on tomorrow's evening tide. Forget me. I have harmed you enough. I'll not have your unhappiness on my conscience."

"Say no more, Captain," she said bitterly. "I understand well enough you do not wish to be burdened with me."

"Aye, lass, if you'll have it plainly spoken, not by you or any wench."

"Will you do me one favour?"

"If I can."

"Do not come near me after this. Let the men row me ashore. I—I do not wish to meet you again—ever."

He stooped and kissed her hand. She heard him cross the cabin and slam the door heavily on his departure, then she cowered down in the bed and gave way to the great rending sobs which threatened to tear her apart.

🕮 Sixteen

SIR WILLIAM STYLES presented himself hurriedly at the inn when summoned by one of the ostlers.

"My dear, I came immediately I knew you were in Lynn. I hear you are unattended. Is something wrong? Is Sir Robin not home?"

She lied as convincingly as she could: "I came seeking you and Miguel. We missed him on the road. I hoped to see the Queen. I . . . I heard—"

"My dear, I would I could give you happier news. There was an accident. Miguel was aboard *The Isabella*."

"They told me. I—did not know what to do, nor did I know where you lodged. Teresa sent the ostler to enquire."

"There is nothing further to concern you. I'll move into this inn and escort you home tomorrow."

"Please, oh please, Sir William—now, at once."

He hesitated. "You're sure you are fit enough, not too upset? Very well, if you wish it. I'll hire a carriage. God knows they are not fit for your use."

"I would rather ride."

"But—"

"I can do so, if the mount is docile and you lead me. I prefer it."

He squeezed her hands gently and went out of her chamber to issue the necessary orders. Carlotta was thankful she did not have to meet Teresa's accusing eyes. The old woman had asked no questions when she had come to the master's cabin on board *The Kestrel*, but her shrewd reasoning must have told her the cause of her mistress's distress. As in the old days when Carlotta had been the child and she her nurse, Teresa soothed and kissed her, finally watching by her until she slept.

In silence, she had dressed Carlotta in the gown provided by the Captain's orders and they had talked only of trivialities on the way to Lynn. The innkeeper received Carlotta with marked respect, almost obsequience. She knew she could rely on him to hold his tongue about the previous day's events. He had informed Sir William Styles that the blind Spanish lady had arrived yesterday past noon with her attendant enquiring for the Spanish gentleman who had so tragically died on the Spanish ship which had caught on fire then exploded just outside the harbour. The Queen had come specially to board her and had been so concerned that an immediate enquiry had been set afoot as to the cause of the accident. Gunpowder stored in the holds, they said, but how did the fire start? The lady also requested to know the whereabouts of Sir William Styles and he had been unable to offer such information. He had provided her respectable accommodation for last night, where she had stayed in comfort, he assured Sir William. In the meantime the town had been in a ferment what with the Queen's visit and the terrible accident, so it was not until today that his ostler had been able to find the honoured gentleman.

Sir William had believed him. He was concerned for Carlotta's bereavement. He had known how she and her cousin had been in sympathy during the voyage on *The*

Isabella, naught improper, of course, but understandable that she had then turned to one of her own countrymen for company.

He put down her distraught condition to her natural feelings and her desire to be safe at home seemed natural enough. He spared her the details and made all speed to return her to her husband's house.

Martha received her with tearful gratitude that her prayers were answered. Despite the fact that the young groom had assured her that Mistress Mallory had chosen to ride to Lynn with Don Miguel's party, she had expressed doubts as to her mistress's safety.

In the parlour she drew Carlotta to the comfort of the fire for today was decidedly chilly, ordered refreshment for Mistress Mallory and Sir William and briskly set about arrangements for his accommodation in the house for he had given way to Carlotta's entreaties to remain with her for some days.

"Martha?" Carlotta called to the housekeeper who checked her exit with a jangle of the keys on her belt. "Has there been no word from the master?"

"No, madam, though we expect him almost hourly and I was distracted as to how I was to explain your absence."

"I see. Fortunately I shall now be able to explain matters."

"And Don Miguel? Will he be returning here, madam?"

"Don Miguel is dead, Martha." Carlotta's voice quivered. "There was an accident. You will hear more of this later. Now I am too worried and upset to talk about it."

"I'm right grieved to hear that. He was a pleasant young man even if he was a Don and a papist."

Sir William felt impelled to dismiss the woman before she further distressed his niece.

"See that my groom is accommodated. He'll take charge of the horses. Let your mistress rest in private now. Teresa will lie down in her room. I think the journey has been a strain on her."

"Aye, sir. Trust me to attend to everything."

Carlotta said little as she ate under the watchful eye of Sir William.

"You fear your husband's censure?" he said gently.

"No, Robin rarely forbids me to do anything I choose to do. It is just that I dread any further reference to Miguel's death. Will you explain and—" her voice cracked piteously, "there was talk of treachery—if it was so, make light of it. He was my kinsman."

"Aye," Styles was clearly uncomfortable, "there *has* been gossip. Walsingham's men have combed the town for strangers. I can scarce believe Don Miguel to have been involved in aught dishonourable. After *The Isabella* struggled on to Dunkirk I became well acquainted with both him and Don Pedro, whose integrity·and courage I admired in misfortune."

"It *was* an accident? You believe that?"

"It is best if we accept it. Naught is to be gained by stirring a hornet's nest."

She excused herself later and with Martha's help retired to her chamber. Teresa was clearly exhausted and the housekeeper assisted Carlotta to undress and climb into bed. She appeared not to be surprised by the disordered gown and Carlotta could only surmise that it was less flamboyant than the one she had been formerly offered on board *The Kestrel*.

She was worn out with restrained tears and physical exertion and left to herself, fell almost instantly asleep.

She woke with a start knowing instinctively that there was someone else in her room though she distinguished no sound in the blackness.

"Martha, Teresa?" She sat up and reached out tentatively. Both her hands were imprisoned and a well-loved voice spoke her name.

"Softly now, my love, there's naught to fear."

"Robin—why didn't they wake me?"

He drew her close and she nestled against the familiar strength of his shoulder.

"They told me how tired you were."

"You know—about Miguel?"

"Aye, sweeting. Sir William told me."

"When did you arrive?"

"Only about two hours ago. I swallowed a hasty meal, and came in here to watch my sleeping wife."

She gave a little sigh. "You are not angry that I left Priors Mallory without your permission?"

"Not angry, just concerned that you might have run into danger."

"Miguel was returning to Spain. It was a sudden whim. I had to bid him good-bye."

"But you did not meet with him in Lynn?"

Did she detect a questioning note in his voice, a sharper lift as though he doubted her relationship with her dead kinsman.

"No." How many times must she lie before this whole incident would fade from her mind or would it ever do so? "I was too late. He went on board. Some seamen heard there was trouble and tried to prevent him. He feared for Don Pedro perhaps, and the ship went up in a sheet of flame." She shuddered and he kissed the top of her head.

"You must forget. Naught good will come from brooding over this. Now, my love, will you call Teresa, rise and dress for I did not come back alone."

He placed a light hand on her lips as she was about to question the identity of the visitor. "Our guest is resting. You will meet Mr. Howard at dinner."

Carlotta had expected the new arrival to be elderly. She was puzzled when he addressed her in a grave, youthful voice.

"I am honoured, Mistress Mallory." He raised her fingers to his lips. Dinner was a pleasant meal, for Sir William and Sir Robin had much to discuss and Mr. Howard spoke informatively of York, where he had recently lived. Carlotta discovered he was a friend of long standing and she surmised that he was connected with one of the old Yorkist families of which Robin had spoken to her earlier.

They retired early. Sir William expressed himself

weary and Carlotta had had little rest for the last three days.

When the house was silent, Robin left her for a time and returned with their visitor.

"I will leave you with Father John and go into the room next door. Teresa is close. Call when you wish us to enter."

Carlotta dropped to her knees as the grave young priest extended his hand in blessing.

"Sit, child, you are not yet recovered from your ordeals. Robin has told me of your need. I can remain for a little time in this house but we must be careful."

"Father, it has been so long since I received the sacrament."

"I know it. God knows your heart and will forgive your lapse."

"Father, confess me. I have sinned greatly."

"My child, we all sin. Do not judge yourself too harshly."

"Are we truly alone? None can hear?"

"Sir Robin is too far away. You can safely reveal what is troubling you."

It seemed that her burden could at last be shared and she whispered the story in pitiful, broken phrases.

He was silent for a while and she waited for his just anger.

"Must I tell my husband, Father?"

"What occurred was against your will. Is that not so? You did not go with this man willingly."

"No, Father—but—"

"But—he stirred you and you responded to his love-making and found it not unpleasing."

"The sin of lust was in my heart. My body desired him."

Again he made no reply but considered. She gave a little dry sob.

"I will give you penance and grant you absolution. I do not consider you wicked, child. You were in anguish and hardly knew what you were about. You must consider deeply about revealing this incident to your husband." He weighed his words carefully. "Normally I would counsel confession. In this case naught good would come from it but to relieve your conscience. Sir Robin would suffer deeply and the shedding of blood might result. Pray earnestly, my child. The Virgin will give you strength to do what is right. Tomorrow I will celebrate Mass in the small chamber at the end of this corridor. Sir Robin will bring you and Teresa when it is time. Be very cautious. You hold my life in your hands."

He blessed her once more and she heard his even tread across the room. She had knelt for his blessing and she rose and climbed into bed. While she waited for Robin to return she lay back against the pillows and thought about Father John's words. If she told Robin the truth it would destroy his faith in her and his happiness. He had given her everything. With one or two words she could turn his love to contempt.

He came to her, padding silently across the room and the first she knew was that he had drawn her into his arms. She fought a wish to hold back herself, to resist him. Now she was aware of instinctive fear and she had to force herself to accept his caresses. He was as gentle and protective as ever.

"Oh Robin, I do love you, I do."

"My love, I know it."

"You spoil me." The words once said she could have bitten off her tongue.

Again he laughed. "And who has revealed the truth to you?"

"I know it, in my heart. Perhaps, soon I will give you a child."

"There is time yet."

"How will I care for him, Robin, as I am?"

"As you do the other things you have learned, sweeting. I have no fears."

She lay at peace by his side. His arm lay gently on her breast. She ran her fingers along its length and he stirred, no steel-hard clamp to hold her tight to his body, imprisoned, possessed and consumed. A little shiver ran through her. Always it would be like this. *He* would lie by her side, a silent ghost to remind her not that she had felt utter fear and helplessness in his clasp but that he had stirred in her something which would never be forgotten. One part of her burned for his touch and the thought filled her with self-disgust. She lay for a long time listening to Robin's steady breathing, then her body's weariness took its toll at last and she slept.

When Robin woke her it seemed that the night could not have passed so quickly, and that she had slept only seconds.

"I would let you rest but Father John must not be about his work when the household is stirring."

"Robin," Carlotta sought to detain him. "Will you not attend mass with me?"

"My love, I must keep watch. No one else can be trusted completely."

She knelt with Teresa while the priest went through the sacred rite. Its magic stole over her, renewing her, restoring her peace. Afterwards there were tears in her eyes as she bent to kiss his fingers and he blessed her again.

"Keep your faith unsullied. Do not confuse religion with the policies of men who use the faith as a shield or spur to further lust for power."

She was relieved that he had touched upon the source of her distress. Miguel had planned murder in the name of his faith. The remembrance had shamed her trust. This priest's censure of such unworthy conduct, even of those most powerful, touched her. Her beliefs could be kept safe and pure, and she reached for Teresa's guiding hand to lead her from the room. Through a haze of tears she felt a flash of golden light. For a second the impulse failed to register in her conscious mind, then she stopped in her walk to the door, turned back to the priest and blinked her eyes rapidly. She had not been deceived. Faintly, so very faintly, she could perceive a glimmer—a sheen of light or gold from the crucifix he had surely placed on the improvised altar. She felt the anxious pressure of Teresa's hand on her arm, then turned again and resumed her walk. It was too soon yet to tell. In the past there had been greyness, a suspension or the lessening of her utter darkness. Now there was hope. Later she would ask Robin to summon Martyn Hartington. Perhaps he would know more. For the present she would keep this to herself.

If Sir William suspected the reason for Mr. Howard's visit to Priors Mallory he showed no sign of it. The young man was an agreeable companion and after breakfast professed himself eager to examine the contents of Sir Robin's library. He had heard much of its fame, he said, and Carlotta gave a wry smile as she mentally envisaged the twinkle in his eye. Robin's interests in alchemy and the astronomers might well be construed as rank heresy for the young Jesuit. Robin pressed Sir William to stay with them for at least some days. He accepted but Carlotta knew that Lady Anne's demands would have to be met and he would soon be forced to take his departure though reluctantly. He left them to ride while the weather favoured them. It was cold but sunny enough.

She had expected Robin also to leave her and go about his business on the estate but he lingered in the parlour and she was glad to have his company. Even so there was a restraint between them and she feared he might become as conscious of it as she herself was and blundered into her news more hurriedly than she had intended.

"Today, with Mr. Howard, I had a strange sensation." She paused then, anxious not to raise his hopes and unwilling to put her own into words in case the very voicing of them might bring disappointment. "I could have been mistaken, of course. I was in a receptive state, you will understand, but I thought I saw colour, a gleam of something golden, perhaps the candle flame, or some jewel."

He crossed at once to her side, his voice almost trembling with his own excitement.

"My heart, is it so? Did you tell Teresa, ask if you were right?"

"No—I was afraid to excite her." She hesitated. "This is not the first time. I've glimpsed a kind of grey light before but the state lasts for such a short while."

"Martyn must be consulted. He said such a thing is possible." He caught both her hands and conveyed them to his lips. "Only be patient, my heart. God will hear our prayers. You *will* see again."

She gave a shaky laugh. "Pray do not summon Martyn so hastily. He will think us fools. We cannot be sure I did not imagine the whole incident."

Realising the need to turn her mind from possible disappointment, he turned to other matters, in particular some details of his stay in the North and since they were alone, he told her of Father John Howard.

"He is a Jesuit, as you guessed. His mission is to minister to the Catholic community in England but unlike many, he is committed to no policy against the Queen or State. My contacts have assured me of this and I believe them, otherwise I would not harbour the man. Since the Pope excommunicated our Queen and was foolish enough to encourage those who wish to depose her, life has been almost impossible for priests. They are forbidden to celebrate mass and every second he remains here puts him in danger, so never let yourself be taken off guard in Styles's company. I believe the man to be sympathetic but we dare trust no one."

"I understand."

"Howard cannot remain more than a few days but he has promised to send me another priest later. It might be possible to absorb him into the household in some clerkish capacity."

Martyn Hartington came later in the day when he heard Sir Robin had returned. Robin brought him out to Carlotta where she sat in the knot garden catching the last of the sun.

Martyn greeted her warmly. "I am glad to hear you are safely returned, Mistress Mallory. I was tempted to come in search of you. I hear there is unrest in Lynn."

"Because of the accident on the Spanish ship?"

"Aye." His tone was grave, "But some say it was no accident."

The two men spoke of their concern for the Queen. Carlotta twisted her hands nervously in her lap. Robin prompted her to talk of the morning's experience. Almost unwillingly she told the doctor of that and the one or two previous signs that her blindness might not be so permanent.

"Let us go into the house, lady. I would like to look further into this."

She went obediently and sat tensed in the parlour while Martyn peered intently into both eyes and she recoiled as she had once before at the warmth which told her a lighted candle or taper had been brought close to her pupils, but she saw nothing.

"What do you think, Martyn?" Robin strove to appear casual. "Are we hoping for too much?"

"It is difficult to say. I said at the time I have known of such cases where sight returned. I could not guarantee it. There appears to be no injury to the eyes themselves. Mistress Mallory sustained several injuries to the face and the back of the head. In all events the returning sight will be very gradual and perhaps only partial."

"If I can see only enough to guide my steps, I should praise The Virgin, or even to distinguish night from day." Carlotta leaned forward eagerly. "Do you think I imagined what I saw?"

He placed one consoling hand on her arm. "I pray not, Mistress Mallory. We can hope, but do not expect results too suddenly."

"As the wounds heal, surely sight will improve." Robin pressed him for further reassurance. "The wound on the temple is healed and there are no marks where that devil struck her. You seem to think the blow on the back of the head caused the mischief."

"It would seem so. Authorities argue on the subject, but I have heard of such blows which had similar effects. I cannot think that the superficial cuts and bruises on the face would be serious enough." He moved from her chair. "I must go, Robin. I'm summoned to the El-kes's farm. The old man is ailing, some constriction of breathing and Elsa will soon be near her time."

"I'll ride with you. I need to see Richard on a busi-ness matter. If you will excuse me, Carlotta. I shall be back well before dinner and Sir William is in the library and will keep you company. Shall I call him?"

"No, no. I shall do well enough. Go with Martyn by all means. I have work in the still-room to occupy me if Martha will assist."

Robin took his leave. She sat still till both men had left the room and she was sure they had also left the house. Her fingers clenched tightly on the chair-arm. It was incredible. She had misheard—she must have done. Had she questioned Robin he would have retracted—

"There are no marks where that devil struck her."

Instinctively she lifted her hand to her cheek-bone. There had been a bruise on the cheek. It had stood out lividly. She recalled holding the candle close to the Venetian glass in the cabin of *The Kestrel* and noting the bluish-purple stain which had marred the whiteness of her skin. It was not to be forgotten—but Robin had not known of the incident. Twice the Captain had struck her—the second time after she had stupidly gone on deck. He had been furious at the need to punish his men for their attack on her. He had lashed out at her, called her wanton—and he had hit her—

Something had prompted her to say nothing of the blow. When Robin found her she had kept silent. At the time she had not known why. Perhaps she had blamed herself and feared that her shame would communicate itself to her rescuer but she knew without one shadow of doubt that Robin had not known—

His words screamed at her in the silence of the room. How had he known? She got to her feet. She must not stay here. She must find some corner where she would not be discovered. There must be time to think out each word, each happening. It was not possible—

At the end of the garden was the seat near the rose

bush, the fatal seat where Miguel had sat and she had overheard his talk with his visitor. Few of the servants knew she could reach so far unaided, but she could, and today she must.

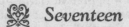 *Seventeen*

IT WAS very quiet at the end of the garden near the wall. She had stumbled her way to the seat and here she felt safe and she gave way to a bitter storm of weeping.

Whatever the truth of the matter Robin had deceived her. He knew far more about the captain of *The Kestrel* than he had disclosed. There was no doubt that unless he had heard of her experiences from other lips than her own he could not have been aware that she had been struck.

This man who had kept her secure, cherished and protected her even from the prying tactlessness of Lady Anne Styles, had lied to her, probably from the first moment he had lifted her from the beach. Had he indeed known that she would be there, even given orders to recover her and keep her at Priors Mallory?

The most terrible thought she would not face, then as the weeping lessened and she forced herself to think out the implications, she knew that it had to be faced and borne. Robin knew of an incident which had occurred when she and *The Kestrel*'s Captain had been almost alone. Unquestionably she had not spoken of it. Had the Captain? It was just possible that he boasted of the blow to another, but unlikely. A man, and *Kestrel*'s Captain, whatever his faults, could not be accused of behaving in a manner less valiantly than the most courageous of men, would not have talked of his attack on a helpless girl. He would have been half ashamed of his action, yet could she now be sure of anything, of motives, reactions, rational behaviour?

She determinedly pressed her mind to accept the inevitable. Robin had been present. He and *The Kestrel*'s Captain were one man.

Once faced, incredible as it seemed, she was less distraught, and she lined up the facts for examination.

Sir Robin had been recently absent from Priors Mallory when she first arrived there. Martha had told her so. He had been with Martyn Hartington in Cambridge, or so the housekeeper believed—but could Carlotta even now trust Martha? The woman had described Robin. Several people had. He was tall, rather stooped, they said, and fair.

The Captain of *The Kestrel* was a big man, tall, she remembered that, but broad, red-bearded. Robin wore no beard, unfashionable even in an Englishman who preferred to vegetate on his country estates. Had Robin shaved off that beard on his return to Priors Mallory? Only recently he had begun to grow one. Before his departure for the North she had commented on the stubbly feel of his chin as he kissed her.

Carlotta's one contact with her husband, at least in early days, was his voice, light, the voice of a scholar, often tinged with an accent of soft mockery.

She shuddered. No, it was impossible that the strong deep tones of *The Kestrel*'s Captain could be so disguised. That voice which had bellowed over the wind and waves and had instantly quelled the rowdiness on the lower deck, could not be the one which had instructed her in chess and entertained her over the accompaniment of the virginals nor whispered the gentle endearments which had delighted her in their love-intimacy.

The voice which had been husky with passion and fury two nights ago, which had laughed at her fear and hysterical pleading, could not be the one of her husband.

She pressed a tightly balled fist to her temple. The

man had been in a fury? Why? He had punished her as
he had that previous time when he thought her guilty of
inciting his men. Did he think her implicated in the plot
against the Queen? If so, why had he not left her to the
tender ministrations of Sir Francis Walsingham's minions?

"Oh, no," she whispered brokenly, "no. I will not believe it, I cannot. Robin—not that."

He had found her in Miguel's arms. Had jealousy
prompted his actions? Her body writhed now as she recalled the terror of their union.

"Your husband has spoilt you." He had tantalised
her in her tearful pleading, then later, his anger sated,
"I'm sorry. Events have stirred me."

What events? His belief that she betrayed him with
Miguel?

She fought back rising panic. If she accepted the
stark ugliness of the facts, what then? The attack on her
life in Cambridge. There had been no play-acting in the
little room. Even now she could feel the intruder's
closeness, the rank stink of his breath. He had meant
murder. She had put out a hand and felt the velvet of
his sleeve—Robin's sleeve? She gave a choked cry. If it
had been so, he had not finished her then. One blow
would have silenced her before the leap through the
window. It would have been easy. But he had not killed
her and later a man had been found murdered—Peter?
Robin had denied it—but nothing made sense any
longer.

Sir Robin Mallory was a respected Norfolk gentleman. The Queen trusted him, favoured him, unusually
so, since he made no secret of the fact that his allegiance was not formally given to the House of Tudor.
He would be desperate to protect his name and property. Accused and found guilty of piracy he would hang
at Tyburn, so how could he ensure that this Spanish
woman would not destroy his peace?

Carlotta tried to judge his actions. He had left her on
board, secure in the cabin, he believed, but she had escaped with Peter's connivance and when pursued, been

badly injured. That had been due to no action of his. He had abandoned her on the beach, blind, helpless, yet if all this were true—why, why had he rescued her later or had he not expected her to be found by the fishermen and drowned on the incoming tide? She tortured herself with the thought. No wonder Peter had fled from his anger and joined the Players company. Faced with the likelihood of Peter warning her against him, he had put the boy out of harm and been forced to prevent her hearing the truth.

There was no denying that the facts combined to a horrifying reality. Robin had on his hands a blind girl who could bring about his death with one little thoughtless word. The Queen had urged him to marry her. Was there not safety in that? He had obeyed and brought her back to Priors Mallory. At first there must be no ugly whispers. No accident must happen yet—but what had he in store for her?

Did he love her at all? If he did not, he had had a second chance to dispose of her on board *The Kestrel.* He had not taken it.

She was suddenly aware of the need for deliberate action. There were others who could identify *The Kestrel's* Captain and she must know the truth without shadow of doubt. The household at Priors Mallory might well know of its master's activities and be perfectly prepared to protect him, or they too might be as unaware of them as the Queen's officers. Hartington could not be trusted either. From the first she had suspected his easy fluency in her tongue and his calm acceptance of her helplessness. One other man had been on board *The Kestrel,* had seen its Captain as she had, Sir William Styles.

She made her way from the seat near the wall and called for assistance when she entered the knot garden. Immediately the gardener's boy came to guide her into the house.

"Thank you, Tom, I can find my way now. Is Sir William Styles in the house?"

"I think so, mistress. Shall I look for him?"

"If you would. Tell him I'll be in the parlour."

As she crossed the hall she was hailed by her quarry. "Carlotta."

"Sir William," she turned to him thankfully. "Thank God I found you so quickly. Please come into the parlour."

She flung open the door and listened. The room was empty, but she groped for Sir William's sleeve. "Are the servants away from this part of the house?"

"Assuredly. Martha and the maids are busy above stairs and the boy who just went by me is the only man-servant in the house."

She drew him inside, her customary good manners deserting her in her need.

"Robin has not yet returned?"

"No, I—"

"Thank God. Sir William, I must speak to you urgently."

"My dear, if there is something wrong I think you should wait—"

"My news can't wait. I know the identity of the Captain of *The Kestrel*."

"Carlotta."

"It is Robin, my husband."

There was shocked silence. When Sir William's answer came it was guarded.

"Carlotta, what fool has told you such a lie? That is impossible."

She swung round to face him and put up a hand to touch his face. He clasped her searching fingers and, since she was insistent, carried them to his cheek.

"You are not trembling. You are honest?"

"What do you mean, child? If I do tremble it will be with shock. Did you think I lied?"

"You saw him—the Captain?"

"Only a short time in the cabin."

"You would know him again."

He paused deliberately. "I could not swear to do so, but the man was a stranger—"

She interrupted him ruthlessly. "I believe it was Robin."

"But—"

"I have proof. Robin has spoken to me of happenings known only to that man and there are other things—"

She broke off uncertainly as Sir William squeezed her fingers excessively hard.

"What is it? Is Robin—?"

"I apologise for my unheralded entry, Mistress Mallory, but Sir William was about to introduce me. Unfortunately he had no opportunity. May I bid you 'Good day' and carry greetings from Her Grace, The Queen."

"Sir Francis—" Carlotta paled and Sir William held her tightly. She pulled herself together determinedly. "Robin has ridden out on business concerning the estate. Pray, sit, sirs. I can find my own chair. Is there wine, Sir William? If not, please ring for attendance. If there is, will you pour for Sir Francis? I fear you must be wearied, sir."

While she prattled polite trivialities her mind raced with the enormity of her disclosure. Walsingham—here, and with what purpose? Had he heard? Of course he had. The man was like a falcon trained for the slightest sight and sound of his prey, but what had he made of her talk? Until she was certain, she had not the wish or responsibility of acquainting the Queen's officers with what was only surmise. Sir William had attempted to halt her half hysterical accusations. Why had she been such a fool? She had not waited for him to assure her that they were alone. Walsingham had apparently met Sir William in the courtyard and entered close behind him. From the first, he had been present and how could he fail to understand? He himself had questioned her most carefully about *The Kestrel* in the Queen's own presence chamber.

He appeared to ignore the damning consequences of her words and spoke his errand civilly enough.

"You bloom delightfully here in the good Norfolk air, Mistress Mallory. I hope Sir Robin is as well."

"In excellent health, I thank you, sir. He has been in the North."

"Indeed? He has friends there?"

"I believe so." She stiffened at his note of interest.

"I thought I saw a figure near a window above, not a servant."

"That will be Mr. John Howard. He stays with us for the present, Sir Francis." Carlotta tensed herself for their talk. Now she held the priest's life in her hands as well as Robin's. Had rumour of Father John's presence in the house brought Sir Francis from Lynn? She must watch her words carefully from now on.

Sir William closed her fingers over a wine goblet. The pressure of his grip silently warned her to be cautious and to drink. She needed the warmth and fire of the wine.

"What is your business in our part of England, Sir Francis? I do not flatter myself that, busy as you are, you are here to satisfy yourself about our health."

"Mistress Mallory. I would this were but a social call."

"Pray, sir, what news have you then for us?"

"I regret I must take your husband from you for a while."

Her hand jerked and Sir William came to her side as she stumbled out an apology through stiffened lips. He stooped and wiped the split wine from her gown.

"Forgive me, I am still stupidly clumsy. Sir Francis's words surprised me."

Walsingham's suave tones expressed regret.

"I am grieved that I alarm you. You will know there has been disturbance and concern in Lynn. It is merely that the Queen is anxious for all loyal gentlemen in the area to present themselves at court. We need Council to hear evidence and consider future action. I am sure Sir Robin will wish to comply with the Queen's request. I come personally out of friendship to ask for his help. I hope he will not deny me."

"You can be certain he will not."

Carlotta's fingers tightened in Sir William's clasp as

her husband answered for himself from the doorway. "Sir Francis, it is good to see you. I am sorry there was delay before I was informed of your arrival. I see my wife has made you welcome to Priors Mallory."

"Very welcome." The Queen's secretary of State bowed his answer to his host's greeting.

"You will stay our guest tonight?"

"I must decline, sir. My need to be in London is urgent. I would wish to begin my journey almost immediately."

Sir Robin was utterly calm. "I understand. Do you wish me to go with you?"

"I would be glad of your company. My men await me in the yard. If you prefer—"

"No, man. If the Queen has need of me, why the Queen shall have me immediately."

"The Queen knows well and loves those who serve her so excellently."

Robin came to Carlotta and stooped to kiss her. "My deepest regret, my heart. Sir Francis and I will ride hard. I must leave you here. Sir William will stay until I send word. May I rely on you, sir?"

"You may."

"My grateful thanks. I will see that my saddle-bag is packed only with necessities. Excuse me, my dear."

She sought to stay him, to convey some warning of the disaster to come, but his kiss was but hurried and, talking of affairs, he drew Sir Francis from the room. Sir William kept her still in the chair, his fingers pressing hard into her shoulders.

"Be quiet, niece. Stay where you are."

"He knows." She gave a harsh, dry sob.

"What does he know? There is no proof."

"Why should he arrest Robin?"

"Arrest? Who said aught of arrest?"

"Sir William, that man is armed and will suffer no denials. His officers are in the courtyard. He takes Robin, willing or no."

"Possibly—possibly—"

"On what charge?" She was desperate for reassurance. "He cannot think Robin implicated in the affair in Lynn."

"I think not." Sir William's tone was thoughtful. "He is undoubtedly extremely interested in your visitor upstairs."

He made no comment as she trembled violently under his hold.

🎍 *Eighteen*

FOR THE second time in months Carlotta found herself in an ante-room of the Queen's presence chamber in an agony of apprehension. Sir William Styles stood close beside her and she could hear the angry slap-slap of Martyn Hartington's shoes as he paced the room.

"Hartington, come and be still, man. You wear yourself out needlessly and you are distressing Carlotta. It's not like you to be so disturbed in an emergency. We have been granted audience, that in itself is promising. The Queen is in Council. These are troubled times."

Hartington checked his pacing. "Forgive me, Carlotta. I am not making this easy. You will recollect, sir, that the Queen has agreed to receive Mistress Mallory, not either of us. We can do nothing but wait."

"Martyn, will you not trust me?"

"*Can* we trust you, madam?" His question was blunt and her cheeks flamed.

"I will save Robin if it is possible."

"And if it is not?"

"Then the man will die," Styles snapped. "Face facts, doctor. Sir Robin Mallory has committed acts of piracy. He has disobeyed the Queen. Is it likely that she will be magnanimous? She is not famed for such conduct."

"He serves the Queen with his wealth, his reputation, his life. If there were not men like Hawkins and Drake and Mallory, how long would she have remained on her throne, and how long would England be Protestant?"

Styles gave an embarrassed grunt and Hartington reached down and touched Carlotta's cold fingers. "Forgive me. I hurt you further. It is just that you have little cause to plead for him and his life depends on you now. None of his friends can save him. If she wishes to throw him to the wolves—to appease those mealy-mouthed hypocrites who counsel peace at all cost, he hangs at Tyburn."

"I love him, Martyn. Will you not believe that?"

Carlotta had learned patience during the wearisome hours that she had fought her way to this ante-chamber. In those hours she had time to consider, to probe her feelings, to know whatever it cost her in shame, or dignity, she would crawl on her knees into the Queen's presence if need be to plead for Robin's life.

Sir William had forced her to remain silent until Robin had left with Sir Francis Walsingham. She had no opportunity of speaking with her husband, or demanding the answer to the one question that burned its way into her brain. Courteously he had taken leave of them and his quiet confidence, conveyed by the tone of his voice, bade her make no objection nor question the manner of his going. Father John's presence in the house was sufficient cause for a charge of treason and it was vital that they all kept calm.

When they were alone she told her pathetic little tale to Sir William, not even sparing herself the sordid facts of her association with Miguel and telling badly of her punishment in the cabin of *The Kestrel*.

"You do not believe me." She challenged his silence.

"I cannot accept that Sir Robin Mallory and this pirate can be one man. I saw him, Carlotta. His voice—manner, God's Teeth, I've eaten with him, ridden with him and—it confounds me."

"One man would confirm or deny the truth of my accusation, Martyn Hartington. I thought you would—I even thought that—" Her voice trailed off. "I thought that you knew."

"You thought it possible I would allow such a man to wed you?"

"I do not know what to believe any more. Can you not understand I love him. I love my husband, yes and *him*. It breaks my heart that he treated me so badly but it makes no difference."

"If what you say is true, he attempted to kill you."

She shook her head helplessly. "That may not be so. I cannot tell."

"The man upstairs, he's a priest?"

She nodded briefly as he shot the question at her. "He is no plotter, I swear it. He too will die horribly if you betray him. Of your charity say naught of his presence here."

Styles grunted. "I thought as much. I've no sympathy with Papists nor have I stomach for the barbarous way some of them have been butchered. God knows I still recall the fires of Smithfield when Protestants burned. I'll not willingly bring that fate on any man who is no danger to this land or the Queen and for his probity I will take your word."

"You think it wise if we counsel him to ride from here today?"

"I think not, that would merely invite suspicion. Let things go on as they are for the moment. In the meantime we'll summon Dr. Hartington."

It proved unnecessary to do so, since Martyn Hartington rode up to the house as the candles were lighted. His face was pale and set. Sir William and Carlotta were about to be served.

She rose immediately, jarring the table clumsily in her haste. "You have heard?"

"Aye, lady. What in the name of God is the reason Walsingham takes Robin so suddenly?"

"Doctor, will you dine with us?" Sir William's voice cut across the young doctor's impatient question and the possibility of Carlotta making an unwise answer. "I am sure my niece is willing to offer hospitality and I think you know Mr. Howard."

Carlotta seated herself more calmly. "Certainly you must stay. Martha, lay another place for the doctor at once. Sir Robin has been summoned to Council. It is irritating that the Queen's need of him should come so soon after his return from York, for I have missed him sorely, but it cannot be mended. When the Queen commands we must obey."

Hartington took the hint and sat down with them. Polite conversation was kept up during the meal and afterwards Howard withdrew to his chamber and Sir William conducted Carlotta and Hartington into the private parlour.

"I have given orders that we shall not be disturbed."

"Did Robin go willingly? Why—" Hartington broke off and the older man put him at ease.

"Speak freely. I know about the priest."

"Walsingham made no effort to arrest him?"

"No. I think he suspects but has no proof. He said he required Robin's presence at the Council. The plot in Lynn was real enough and the local squires have been questioned."

"Then Robin is safe enough?"

"I—I don't know. I talked foolishly without realising Walsingham was there. The man walks like a cat. Sir William attempted to warn me but it was useless."

"You talked of the priest?"

"No." Carlotta swallowed and reached out her hand for Sir William to take it and give his support. "No, of other matters."

"I don't understand."

"Do you not, Dr. Hartington?" Sir William's tone was uncompromisingly blunt. "Did you know that Sir Robin was present in Lynn during the Queen's visit?"

"If he were, it was no business of Walsingham's."

"Then he was." Styles was insistent. Carlotta's fingers trembled in his.

Hartington attempted to retract. "How should I know Robin's whereabouts? I am not in his confidence."

"Are you not, Martyn?" Carlotta appealed to his friendship. "Let us be honest. If what we fear is true, Robin is in peril. Was he in Lynn?"

"I swear he had no hand in the plot against the Queen." Martyn's reply was stiffly delivered.

"He was on board *The Kestrel*."

Carlotta heard the doctor's swift intake of breath and she delivered her body-blow before he recovered. "He *is* its captain. Admit it."

"He told you?"

"Not directly. I am right, Martyn? In the name of the Virgin, do not prevaricate. I told Sir William of my fears. Walsingham heard and will hold this against Robin."

Martyn sat back heavily in a chair near the table. "What use is pretence? Aye, Robin owns *The Kestrel* and captains it on certain expeditions."

"Like the attack on *The Isabella*."

"Yes."

"You were not on board?"

"Not on that particular voyage, no."

"You have always known, doctor, that Robin was responsible for my injuries." Carlotta spoke very softly.

His voice was husky with surprised emotion. "He forbade me to speak of it. He meant you no ill. You were safe enough in the cabin. Why did you leave it? He did not abandon you on the beach."

"Then who did?"

"I don't know. His shock was not assumed. When he summoned me to Priors Mallory he could not account for the episode himself. He had to lie to you. What choice had he? You would have betrayed him."

Carlotta said quietly, "I *have* betrayed him. The question is, what can we do? I must leave for London. The Queen may consent to see me. I—" her voice trembled. "I cannot manage such a journey alone. Teresa will go with me but—"

"I shall accompany you. My niece must be suitably chaperoned." Sir William came to her and placed a comforting hand on her arm.

"Thank you. I did not like to ask but—what will Lady Anne say? She will be angered. Already you have stayed long away from Buckleigh."

There was a grim note of amusement in his voice. "She will say a great deal, but I am beginning to think I need to be master in my own home. I have discovered it can be a rewarding, though troublesome business."

Hartington said thickly, "I wish to go with you. I may be needed."

Carlotta said gently, "I think it unwise, Martyn. At present you do not lie under suspicion but if you are questioned—"

"I must risk that. You will allow me the right."

"If you wish."

"Thank you. Do we go tomorrow?"

Styles said briskly, "There is no point in delay, but arrangements must be made for the priest. On no account must he be found here."

The fine weather gave way to early fog which delayed them and later heavy rain turned the roads to bogs and each night the two women went cold and exhausted to bed. The city was crowded, many of the inhabitants moving back after the summer exodus to escape plague. Sir William had difficulty in obtaining lodgings in Greenwich and the place was poorly provided. He left Carlotta in Hartington's care and went to the palace to request an audience and to obtain what information he could.

He was not sanguine when he returned to the inn.

"The Queen will see you alone, but I warn you the climate at Greenwich is not healthy. She is in a towering rage, I hear. Her Council, and particularly Burleigh, are exhorting her to condemn the Queen of Scots. Without her as a suitable candidate for Elizabeth's throne the Catholics will be less likely to intrigue in such plots. The Guise affair has shocked the country and Walsingham is constantly reminding the Queen of the present threat from Spain."

"Did she receive you?"

"No. I had to wait hours for my answer and you must be prepared to wait."

"Is there news of Robin?"

"He is lodged in the Tower."

"Then he is accused?"

"No specific charges are laid. There are several of the known 'Sea Hawks' with him."

Hartington gave an exclamation. "Robin would not implicate others."

Styles grunted. "I would think not, but—"

"But—"

"There are methods. Man, man, do not disturb the lady."

Carlotta's lips paled. "You hint at torture?"

"I doubt it, lady. The Queen would have to give consent and she favours Robin. Do not give way to undue fear."

"Sir William, she must see me tomorrow, she must." Carlotta broke down at last and sobbed. "We must get Robin from that dread place. You will take me to the palace at dawn. Please—"

"My child, do not give way. You have been so strong, and you need to keep your courage. The Queen has no use for weaklings. The doctor will give you a draught to make you sleep and I will call Teresa."

Carlotta had protested but given way in the end. Sir William was correct. Naught could be done tonight. They all needed sleep. She had drunk of the bitter liquid and slept, though she dreamed throughout the night and several times woke in a cold sweat of terror.

At the palace they had been greeted with courtesy but scant attention. It seemed obvious that members of the Council had been summoned fast.

Margaret Whitton appeared at the door of the Queen's private chamber.

"Mistress Mallory, the Queen will see you now. I will guide you in." She turned to the two men. "The Queen bade me ask you to wait, sirs."

As she drew Carlotta towards the door she muttered, "She is in a rare temper. Be cautious."

Carlotta pressed her former companion's hand gently in a sign that she had heard and was grateful.

The Queen greeted her roughly enough.

"Well, Margaret, are we to wait all day? Bring Mistress Mallory to her stool. Go out and close the door. If Sir Francis Walsingham asks for me, require him to wait. I will not be interrupted until I ring. Do you understand?"

"Yes, madam."

Carlotta waited nervously for the betraying click which told her Mistress Whitton had left. She had curtseyed low and now stood waiting for the Queen to give her leave to speak.

"Well, Carlotta. God knows, child, I have affection for you but I have little time for old friendships. If you must speak do it quickly."

Carlotta sank unto her knees. "Your Majesty, I beg you to listen. My husband is unjustly accused. What Sir Francis overheard was the hysterical outburst of a stupid wife. Robin is innocent."

"He is, is he?"

"Madam, I swear it. Once I had time to question others, I discovered what a stupid conclusion I had drawn. I was mistaken."

"And who is it that swears so stolidly to Robin's innocence?"

"Sir William Styles could not recognise him. He is certain Sir Robin was not the Captain of *The Kestrel* and Dr. Hartington assures me—"

The Queen cut her short. "And you believe them?"

"Yes, Your Majesty."

"You are prepared to swear you were mistaken, that Robin is not guilty of piracy."

"Truly, Your Majesty."

"On a crucifix?"

The sharply put question caught Carlotta unawares. She hesitated, swallowed, then recovered herself. "If you ask it of me, Your Majesty."

"Then you'd be foresworn. Robin is guilty as hell and you know it. Do you take me for a fool?"

"Robin—he—he confessed? You had him tortured—"

"Stuff and nonsense, miss. Why should I have Robin tortured to confess what I already knew?"

"Knew, madam? I don't understand."

"Yes, knew." The Queen mimicked Carlotta's frightened incredulous tone. "Of course, I knew, always knew."

"Then—"

"Get up from your knees, child. Here, let me help you, sit down on the stool. Take my kerchief. If you must sniff do it and get it over. I've no time for you to have the vapours. Now will you tell me why you speed from Norfolk, insist on an audience and then tell me idiotic lies?"

"Your Majesty, forgive me. My husband, is he not under arrest?"

"Not to my knowledge."

"But he is lodged in the Tower."

"Aye, with several others of his partners in crime. I have called a meeting of 'The Sea Hawks'. The palace is crowded. They were offered accommodation in the Lord Lieutenant's apartments."

"Oh, I thought—I thought—" Tears spilled on to Carlotta's fingers and she dabbed at her streaming eyes in a fury of embarrassment.

"It's easy to see what you thought, miss, and what you are prepared to sacrifice for Robin. I think he doesn't know what treasure he took from *The Kestrel*."

"Madam, I do not understand. If—if as you say, you always knew that Sir Robin was a—pirate, why should he wish to kill me?"

The Queen tapped her sharply on the wrist with her fan. "That you must ask yourself, child. If you're fool enough to think he attempted to do so."

"But on the way to Cambridge, the assassin—I thought—"

The Queen considered. "I think Robin knows more about that incident than he is willing to disclose. That you must tax him with. Well, since you are here, you will tell me what stupid fear brought you here to save a man you thought might be a murderer."

"When—when Sir Francis came to Priors Mallory, I had only just found out—"

"That Robin and *The Kestrel*'s Captain were one and the same man?"

Carlotta nodded and shivered as if the first realisation of the shock had come again to shatter her belief.

"He should have told you long ago. I counselled him to do so, but he feared to lose you."

"Then when you advised me to be his wife you were aware that I was marrying a stranger to the real Sir Robin."

"You were marrying half of Sir Robin, shall we say. Oh, there is a poetic side to my pirate, that's real enough. He can be charming and witty and gentle when it suits him and the time is ripe. That is the Robin you wanted and he gave it to you, protected you from the side you feared and hated, the part of Robin that despises Spain and everything that smacks of cruelty and fanaticism, the part which will attack, rob and kill, plunder and hide what is needful for the protection of this realm. Oh, your dower is safe. Robin steals not for his own enrichment, though I'd not condemn him out of hand if he did so. The greater part of *The Kestrel*'s plunder goes to the State coffers that we might build ships and equip them and be prepared. Do you think I am fool enough to accept Philip's assurances? It but suits me to pretend I do. He will attack England. Already Walsingham's spies tell me the Armada is being made ready for the Great Enterprise, the invasion of England, and thank God, and the stout hearts of men like your husband, we are not so ill-prepared."

"Your Majesty, I see well enough now your need to castigate these men in public while you reward them in private—"

"And you think such conduct dishonourable, miss?"

"Madam, it is not for me to judge."

"No, miss, it is not." The grim tone in the Queen's voice had hardened. "You judge Robin, is that it, despite your will to sacrifice your soul for him if need be?"

"He—he—" Carlotta turned from the Queen, her cheeks scarlet. "He deceived me once when—I cannot speak of it but *that* I cannot forgive."

"I'll not believe that, but it's for you to take up with the man himself. You can have him back to dance attendance on you soon enough. One more thing. Before you leave our Presence, Don Miguel, you loved him, were in his confidence?"

"I love no one but my husband."

"But you went to Lynn to meet him—or so my spies tell me."

"For a purpose, madam."

"You knew of the plot?"

"Yes, madam. I overheard by accident." Carlotta's voice trembled. "In my heart I try to forgive Miguel. I pray for him constantly because—because he believed that what he did was for Spain."

"And you are part Spanish."

"I am English now, madam, with all my heart. I think it was for this reason that my father sent me to England. He knew better than I."

"Yet you are a Papist."

"There are Catholics in England, madam, who dearly love its Queen. I beg you, most sincerely, to remember that."

The Queen lifted her hand and gently stroked Carlotta's hair. "Aye, I *do* believe it, child." She sighed. "I have striven for a way of life in England which allows a man to worship as he pleases. God knows I too pray for peace, but there are times when it becomes necessary to turn from the dictates of one's own heart and go the way one is directed for the good of the whole realm. Now, get you gone, miss, and whatever it is lies between your man and you, destroy it. Believe that he loves you well and whatever he did, he did for that love. You are a fortunate woman, Carlotta Mallory, for all your lack of sight. God grant you soon recover it. I pray for that too."

Carlotta rose and curtseyed. "God keep you, madam."

"Tell Sir William to take you to the rose garden and to leave you there. Give me an hour and I'll send your Robin to you."

Carlotta groped for the Queen's hand and kissed those long slender fingers, then she curtseyed low again and moved slowly to the door.

"Straight ahead. Put your hand to the knob. Farewell, Carlotta Mallory. Name your first daughter Elizabeth. You will already have determined on a name for a son. Do not keep us waiting too long. We have need for fine straightlimbed sons and daughters for England."

"I will not forget, Your Majesty." Carlotta undid the door and passed through. Outside she was close to collapse and was thankful for the outstretched hands of Sir William Styles to support her and convey her to a chair.

🙊 Nineteen

SIR WILLIAM was loth to leave Carlotta alone as the Queen commanded, but she was insistent.

When she heard Robin approach she rose hastily, embarrassment in his presence manifesting itself for the first time. Her cheeks flamed at the memory of what had passed between them last in the cabin of *The Kestrel*. The Robin who had held her close at Priors Mallory on his return was a stranger, less real than the man she had known only a few short hours, whose love-making had so terrified and enchanted her that she would never again be the same woman who had left Spain and married Sir Robin Mallory on the Queen's advice.

"Querida." Even the tone of his voice appeared deeper than she remembered it.

"Sir." The little formal word erected the barrier between them.

He stood silent for a moment then reached out and took her by the shoulders, turning her face to his own.

"Don't, don't put me at a distance. That punishment will be more than I can bear."

She gave a little sob. "Robin, there is naught to punish."

"There is, dear heart, there is."

"I love you, everything else is unimportant. Tell me you are safe. I thought my stupid words would cost you your life."

"I feared more than that—that realisation would cost me your love." He drew her down to the wooden bench. "When did you find out?"

"You mentioned that you'd struck me. I didn't tell you that. I kept it secret. I don't know why, perhaps because even then it hurt too much that you should do so—too much to tell others." She paused and looked away, then as he gently turned her chin back towards him, she continued, "I could not believe it, not after—after that last time. I tried to work it out—then I knew there were so many things. I knew why I sinned in my heart in wishing to remain with *The Kestrel*'s Captain while I still loved Robin Mallory—and even then I could not understand—"

"What, my heart?"

"Robin, if the Queen has always known, and she has, why the attack in Cambridge? She did know. I thought that attempt on my life was to stop me talking but it was not. Even now I cannot think—"

"Querida, it *was* to stop you talking—not to the Queen, to me."

"To you?"

"Adam, my mate, led the attack on the cabin and pursued you in the long-boat. When he knew you were injured he took you near to Lynn and abandoned you on the beach since he dare not leave you to talk in the cabin. Peter was left unconscious on the quay. Adam knew he would have to face a reckoning and he left the ship. Later he joined the Player company. Unfortunately the cabin boy had joined the same group."

"But Peter was not afraid of you. Why did he leave the ship?"

"But Peter *was* afraid of me, very much afraid. When he came to his senses, you were gone. He had no idea what had happened, if indeed you were alive. He felt responsible. He'd engineered the escape, put you in danger. He dared not face me. When both of them saw you, it was a threat to their lives. Peter tried to warn you Adam was in the company. Adam tried to silence you."

"You killed him?"

"Yes."

She shuddered and he held her very close. "Oh Robin, I thought—I thought—".

"That I had tried to kill you."

She nodded, biting her lip.

"Do not concern yourself about Peter. He's safe enough in London. I provided for him but I too needed to silence him. I could not let him blurt out the truth. I wasn't ready to tell you what might have cost me my happiness."

"I think I can understand. That first day on the beach, was it accidental, finding me?"

"Yes, by the mercy of God. When the fishermen called me I could not believe my eyes. I'd left you safe in the cabin, I was, of course, ashore arranging to take you to Priors Mallory. Your presence on the ship was entirely unexpected and it was inconvenient to say the least to find Styles, and Don Miguel Hernandez, King Philip's representative, on board with a gallant and lovely lady who could betray me with one word to the Queen's officers. I tried delaying tactics. If I could keep you at Priors Mallory for some time, perhaps Styles would be unable to present you at Court. I did not expect to love you."

"When, when did you first love me, Robin?"

"I think that first time on *The Kestrel* when I knew you were in danger from my men. I was sure when I saw how you faced up to your blindness. Then my true punishment began. I could not risk losing you. You turned to me in your need, trusted me. Several times I thought to tell you. Before Lady Styles came to Priors Mallory, once on the road to Cambridge but you seemed so happy. After the attack, it was too late."

"Then you found me with Miguel."

"Aye, that was when my control snapped. I had protected you, spoiled you, and all reason went."

"You had been too considerate, my Robin. I am not a child. You might have gone on treating me as one. Perhaps Miguel served us well. In that knowledge I have yet another reason to pray for him."

"He was truly a brave man. The Queen tells me why you went with him to Lynn. God show him mercy, aye, and Don Pedro."

"The Queen says the Spaniards will come."

"Aye, but we are ready." He put his arm round her waist and drew her to him. She gave the ghost of a smile. Once before he had held her tight against his body in this hard, demanding grip. Now she felt the strength and protection of that arm and nestled close.

"When will you take me home?"

"Tomorrow. The Queen has dismissed us until there is need. We shall have warning. The beacon fires will blaze over England, then I shall leave you for a little time and become again the Captain of *The Kestrel*."

He bent and kissed her head. "The Queen gave me a further command."

She hid her crimsoning face against his shoulder. "I know it."

"You are in honour bound to obey the Queen." He chuckled. "I would I could obey all her orders with so good a will. Come, my love, let me take you to your lodgings and later I'll join you there. My quarters in the Tower are a trifle grim and remind me that I might indeed have languished there more fearfully. I hear you were all concerned to rescue me from such close confinement."

He drew her gently to the garden gate. For one moment the sun came out and touched the autumn browns and golds with a burnished glory. She lifted her face to feel its faint warmth.

"God grant you see it soon, my darling," he said huskily.

Her answering smile was as serene as it was confident. "I shall be patient and if your prayers are answered, I shall perhaps see my first child, but if it is God's will that I shall not, I know that I shall have my husband's strength and love to protect us both, and it will be enough."

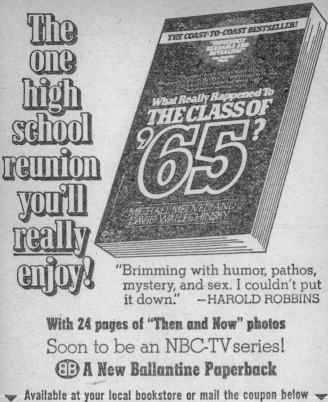